THE TOYMAKER'S CASTLE

ALSO BY PHYLLIS ANN KARR

The Frostflower Series

Frostflower and Thorn (1980)
Frostflower and Windbourne (1982)

The Oz Series

The Gardener's Boy of Oz (1988)

Fantasy Novels

The Idylls of the Queen (1982)
Wildraith's Last Battle (1982)
At Amberleaf Fair (1986)
The Follies of Sir Harald (2001)
The Gallows in the Greenwood (2002)

Romance Novels

My Lady Quixote (1980)
Lady Susan (1980)
Meadowsong (1981)
Perola (1982)
The Elopement (1982)

THE TOYMAKER'S CASTLE

PHYLLIS ANN KARR

A 'Babes in Toyland' Story

Being not quite a fairy tale, retold by Phyllis Ann Karr

Based on the original book and lyrics by Glen MacDonough

WILDSIDE PRESS

For Victor Herbert's Babes in Toyland

Published by Wildside Press LLC.
wildsidepress.com

INTRODUCTION

In early childhood, I once had to turn off a telecast of Babes in Toyland, either because it was time for Christmas dinner, or because all the grown-ups (who were in the numerical majority) wanted to watch something else. Chances are overwhelming that it was yet one more adaptation; but had I been able to watch it through, I would likely have assumed I had seen it, and let it be subsumed in the banks of my unexamined memories. As it was, I spent much of my life in spurts of trying to learn the story I had missed seeing. Now at last, in the year 2019, thanks to a novelette-ization by James Howe (actually published in 1986, but only discovered and acquired by me ca. 2018) and the Internet, I have found as much, perhaps, of Glen MacDonough's 1903 libretto as is still available. And found it worth having waited a lifetime to learn: A story that fairly demanded I back-burner other projects long enough to live with it in the intimate relationship of retelling.

Surely the twentieth century produced no story more ill-used and misrepresented by its multitudinous adaptations than Babes in Toyland, which is why I chose an alternate title for my version. Because what works on the stage doesn't necessarily work on the page (and vice versa), mine is perforce still another adaptation; but one of which I hope MacDonough would have approved. I have incorporated as much as I could of MacDonough's 1903 dialogue, and striven above all to keep both the basic story and the spirit of the original operetta as I read it: A melodrama not of childhood, for all its Mother Goose trappings and vaudeville-style humor, but of that even more painful and magical, frightening and mystical time of life when childhood merges into adulthood, when we remain a little bit fearful lest the "real" grown-ups (i.e., those with more years' experience at it) may find us out for the children we still feel like. I hope and pray that most of us have only to learn that our beloved adult authority figures have faults and foibles just as we do, not that they have been trying all along to destroy us.

CHAPTER I

"Are they really going to put you to death?"

"I'm afraid so," Alan said, nervously adjusting the slightly frayed purple neckcloth he had affected in his attempted disguise as aesthetic literary man J. Egbert Flaffingdale. (It would have worked, too, except...) "Unless a widow marries me."

"And I'm the only widow for ever so far around. Unless there had been a married man killed when the dear old Toymaker's castle burned down, but everybody says there wasn't. Only the dear old Toymaker and his toys."

Alan suppressed a shudder. "Yes. They say I'm to blame for that—"

"Oh, dear, are you? I couldn't ever marry anyone who killed our dear old Master Toymaker and burned up his nice castle and toys."

"But I didn't. I was trapped there completely innocent, and almost burnt up myself." Leave it at that. Don't disillusion her—poor child—about the "dear old" Master Toymaker. "You can't have been a widow for very long."

"No. My first husband fell into the threshing machine and was all threshed up, poor dear man. Of course the machinery was—defective, that's the word they used in Master Toymaker's official report—and the man who put it together wrong ran away so he wouldn't be executed."

Lucky fellow! Alan thought. He made it.

But the very young widow was going on, "My dear Horace was a rich farmer, very rich. His money is paying for my music lessons, so I can be a great opera singer." She warbled off the soprano's famous aria from Korfalottski's Cudmilla and the Bronze Slipper. Alan let her sing it all the way through. She sang very well. And he was in no special hurry.

"There!" she cried as she finished. "Oh, I wish poor dear Horace could have heard me! He would have been so proud of the lessons his money is buying me. I still have plenty of it, you know. Money. If I married you, you wouldn't go and squander it on anything else but my music lessons, would you?"

"We have money of our own, my sister Jane and I." If they ever got it out of their Uncle Barnaby's clutches. "And you have a fine voice. I love listening to it."

She giggled. "Oh, that's just what poor, dear Horace always told me. But you'll have to do more than just listen. Horace always said that if I ever married again, it should never be to anyone else except a first-rate tenor who would sing the great operas with me on the stage."

Alan was taken aback. He had never had a minute of operatic training and, while the whole Piper clan, the Gypsies, and the Toylanders who had watched Marmaduke's show seemed to like hearing him sing, his voice could be called—even now, years after it had broken—a "scrambled baritone."

Meanwhile, the very young and very musical widow was warbling on, "And you'll look very well with me up there on the stage, too, even if you are almost as old as my poor, dear Horace was."

Alan was only twenty-one. But Mrs. Horace must have married the late poor, dear Horace very young indeed—she couldn't be more than seventeen as a widow.

Reminding himself that he had too much in hand to die just now... there was squaring accounts with Uncle Barnaby, making sure that Jane, at least, got the money their parents had left them... and maybe, just maybe, Contrary Mary might not be lost to him quite forever... Alan prevaricated. "Yes, I've sung all the principal tenor roles, though never with a soprano as young and lovely as you."

"Oh!" Her eyelids fluttered. "Let's try one together now! Let's try... the great duet from Melitonsky's Briar Rose! That's my very favorite."

"I'm afraid I'm not in the best voice today. The fire at the Toymaker's castle, you know, and being arrested and falsely charged with starting it, and sentenced to death, and all. It kind of takes it out of a fellow. You'll just have to take my word for my voice."

Mrs. Horace pouted. "A true artist is never put off by anything. No, I could never enter lightly into marriage. You must sing me something first."

"All... right... Do you know the aria in F flat from... from The

Wooden Nickel, by Kipdebeetsky?"

"No!" Her eyes shone with the delight of something new. "I've never even heard of Kipdebeetsky."

Neither have I, Alan thought, even while he told the diva in training, "One of the most popular composers of Paflagonia." Then he launched into a mixture of notes sung to nonsense syllables made up on the spot. It sounded more or less foreignly (or forlornly) operatic to him, but soon sent the poor young widow from the cell in tearful flight.

And she was the only widow to be had! Alan sat down shakily on the cell's one stool (which, no doubt after long application and diligent practice, managed to wobble with only three legs) and would have given himself to furious last-minute meditation if at that same very last minute his old acquaintances Gonzorgo and Roderigo hadn't come in—no doubt to lead him back through the Courthouse to the town square for execution.

It might still be just a little premature to see his life flash past, but not by much. And in a few minutes he would be too busy dying to enjoy it, so he just let it unroll before his eyes now.

CHAPTER II

First, just a glimpse of Father—which surprised Alan, who thought he had been too young to remember Father at all, before he marched off to glorious death on the battlefield—glorious and unexpected, since as a Major-General he should have been far enough out of harm's way. Then a fluster of whites and pastels when Jane was born, and a string of years so happy they would have bored anyone else except the children actually living them. Then solemn doctors in dark trousers when Mother died and the two children, at ages seven and six, were packed off to live with Uncle Barnaby.

They had never known what his first name might be, or maybe his last name. "Barnaby" seemed to do duty for both. But he was their only remaining relative, or at least the only one willing to take charge of two little orphaned tykes (no matter how well behaved), and while he wasn't and could never be Mother, he never—as far as they knew or had ever even guessed, back then—did anything to get in the way of their loving him like an uncle.

If he pinched pennies until the copper squealed for mercy, at least there was always food on the bare table (cheap food, but enough of it); if he didn't believe in wasting fuel, at least there were always plenty of blankets (patched, but warm); and if he was the most law-conscientious landlord ever seen when it came to demanding his rents on time (often remarking that his tenants could afford it, seeing how much more prodigally most of them lived than he did), at least his nephew and niece were always ready to stick up for him whenever the rest of the neighborhood grumbled and complained.

No, all those years of growing up beneath Uncle Barnaby's (sometimes leaky) roof, and they had never even suspected the grumbling and complaining might have any more real foundation than the fact that people just naturally liked to grumble and complain. If Alan and Jane had suspected, it might have buffered the shock.

The Pipers were their earliest playmates in Barnabyville. Almost their only playmates, so it was a good thing there were so many of them. Where most of the town and country was concerned, some of Uncle Barnaby's unpopularity rubbed off on his nephew and niece. But to be fair, the way they stuck up for Uncle Barnaby, the townsfolk must have suspected them of spying for him, telling him about every little improvement Mr. Grundy or Mrs. Hubbard or anybody else made to their homes, so he could raise rents on them. Maybe, even, Alan and Jane actually did some of that, all unsuspecting. But Mr. Piper was probably the richest man in town after Uncle Barnaby—and needed to be, Alan saw now, with fourteen children. With Mr. and Mrs. Piper (Mr. Piper having died just a little more than two years ago) and their maid-of-all-work Hilda Dolittle (who Alan reasoned had that name because she really did so much), it made a crowded household.

Fourteen Piper sons and daughters, seven of each kind. In order of age: Tom and Mary, the twins Jack and Jill, Simon and Bobbie, Peter and Sallie, B.B. and Muffy, Tucker and Curlie, Bobby and Little Red. The last two were still in their rockabye cradles when Alan and Jane came to live with Uncle Barnaby, but Tom Piper was a year older than Alan, and Mary was Alan's own age.

Mary. Dear Mary. Sweet Mary. Contrary Mary. Famous for doing things the wrong way—and getting them done well anyway. She planted orange marigolds beside pink primroses, and her garden still looked beautiful. She sugared her fried chicken and peppered her lemonade, and they still tasted good. When she got old enough, she used lip rouge on her dark eyebrows and blue eyeliner on her lips, and she was still the prettiest girl in town (after Jane, but a fellow's sister didn't count, not that way).

Mary Contrary, who had gone and married Uncle Barnaby!

Only to save him, Alan. As he would have married a widow to keep Mary from having sacrificed herself in vain... and to make sure Jane did all right... and, honestly, because Alan wasn't that fond of being the first to go, just when he was getting a good start on being grown up.

The flash-past of his life reached that August afternoon in Mary's garden when they were sixteen. Her older brother Tom was on the swing across the field, sitting and swinging with Jane while they ate her mother's angel cake and watched the twins Jack and Jill filling their buckets at the well, the younger Piper children tumbling hither and yon in the grass. Alan was starting to feel something for Mary that he guessed might mean he wasn't exactly a kid anymore.

It was the first time he had seen her with blue lips. "Mary," he asked, "are you that cold?"

"How contrary do you think I am, Alan Flinders? To get cold in the middle of a sunny day in August?"

"Because your lips are all blue. So I thought I'd ask if I could kiss 'em and make 'em warm."

"Oh, kiss my asters!" She tossed one at his mouth. "I'm wearing lip rouge."

"I never knew lip rouge came in quite that color."

"Well, it's really Jill's eye liner, but she's still too young to have a make-up box, so Mother took it away from her and gave it to me."

"And you plan to use the real lip rouge on your eyes?"

Mary laughed. "No. Maybe in my eyebrows. But if I used it around my eyelids, it'd make me look like I couldn't sleep at night, or even when people like your Uncle Barnaby bored me."

"Uncle Barnaby isn't boring."

"No, maybe not to you and Jane. In fact, if I were you, and had to live with him, I'd stay as wide awake as I could, all the time."

"Contrary Mary Piper... if you were anybody else... even if you were your brother Tom or Jack or even Simon, I'd hit you for hinting a thing like that about Uncle Barnaby!"[1]

"So you saw what I was hinting." She tossed her head—her bobbed brown curls almost winked at him in the sunlight. "Good for you! But maybe your Uncle Barnaby is the one you should think about hitting. Remember last summer when the scaffolding collapsed under you and Jane while you were helping paint his house? You were lucky to get out of it with no worse than sprained wrists and ankles."

"Our house—Uncle Barnaby's and Jane's and mine, all three. And it was Mr. Franklin's fault, for the bad rope he sold Uncle Barnaby."

"Umpf," said Mary. "More likely Uncle Barnaby was too cheap to buy good rope. Assuming that's all it was. What's really hard to figure out is why he'd ever squander money on paint just to make his house look a little better. And what about that time when you were nine or ten, and he left you two alone in Farmer Brown's field where

1   This was in a time and place when people considered it appropriate sometimes to hit other people for insulting them.

the bull with the twisted horn was?"

"Uncle Barnaby didn't know the bull was there that day! Any more than we did."

"It was posted. Farmer Brown had a big sign posted right up there on the gate."

"Who reads signs? Anyway, when we went in, the bull was clear on the other side of the field, where that ridge hid him, so we just thought Farmer Brown had already taken him in for the day."

Mary repeated "Umpf" and went on, "Well, what about the Christmas dinner he gave you that first year you lived with him—bean loaf and cabbage—" She made a face.

"Uncle Barnaby is a great cook—"

"He has to be. Nobody else would cook for him. Especially not at what he'd be willing to pay them."

"His bean loaf and cabbage are scrumptious!"

"Oh, what a sacrifice for you and Jane to come and eat your Christmas dinners with us Pipers ever since!"

"And we had potatoes that day, too."

"Also wine," Mary pointed out. "And the wine made you deadly sick."

"Well, we were really much too young to be drinking wine—six and seven years old! But Uncle Barnaby couldn't know that. Never drinking wine himself, except when he's under really great stress—"

"He's under great stress quite a bit of the time, to hear his complaints."

"And even then he doesn't, after all, because there's never a bottle in the house."

"And he didn't drink any of the wine he served you that Christmas, either," said Mary. "As I recall the tale."

"Well, how could he? With only that one little bottle, just enough for Jane and me. He wanted to give us a special treat, nice cherry wine."

Mary again repeated, "Umpf," and Alan settled their quarrel by kissing her.

It was the afternoon they knew they were in love.

Coincidentally, it was the same afternoon Jane knew she and Mary's brother Tom were in love. But that confidence came only in the next scene of Alan's life as it flashed past him.

Of course, all those earlier perilous occasions Mary mentioned had already flashed past in their proper order, but not until now, today in the Toyland jail cell, did Alan think, Yes, Jane and I really should have suspected Uncle Barnaby a lot sooner.

CHAPTER III

Alan's life flashed past him so fast that Gonzorgo and Roderigo seemed to have stood there posed midstep from his babyhood glimpse of Father until the day they first came into Alan and Jane's life.

It was only weeks ago, the afternoon he and his sister came in laughing from their last romp with Mary and Tom and the rest of the Piper clan through the crisp autumn leaves, and found two strange men drinking hot water with Uncle Barnaby at his elegantly stark kitchen table.

"Here are the children now," said Uncle Barnaby. He still called them children, even when they were twenty and twenty-one years old. About half the time Alan, and sometimes even Jane, lodged a tiny little complaint about it, but before they could do so today, Uncle Barnaby introduced his visitors as Captain Gonzorgo and Crewman Roderigo of his own ship the Wooden Nickel.

Mr. Roderigo was a portly tall man with thick black hair, bushy black eyebrows, and sentimental lines around his mouth, as if he cried a lot. In fact, the first look they had at him, he was wiping his eyes over his mug of hot water. Captain Gonzorgo was a wiry small man with thin sandy hair, thin sandy eyebrows, and a look as if he never cried at all. Both of them sported big handlebar mustaches and, curiously, Captain Gonzorgo's mustache was as black as Mr. Roderigo's.

"Doesn't Miss Jane look pale to you?" Uncle Barnaby asked the visitors.

"Pale as skim milk," said Captain Gonzorgo, and Mr. Roderigo cried faster than he could wipe away his tears.

"Jane?" said Alan. "She looks fine to me."

"Brothers," said Uncle Barnaby, "are infamous for being the last ones to notice such things."

"For the matter of that," said Captain Gonzorgo, "he looks pretty pale, himself. He'd better come along, too."

"My idea, exactly," said Uncle Barnaby. "That's why I packed both their bags for them. Hurry along with Captain Gonzorgo and Mr. Roderigo, now, children!"

Alan asked, "Hurry along where, Uncle?"

"On a nice, leisurely sea cruise, of course. For your health."

"Oh, Unkey!" Jane cried in delight. "But how much will it cost you?"

Uncle Barnaby drew out his pocket handkerchief and wiped his eyes. (Maybe whatever Mr. Roderigo had was catching.) "If absolutely necessary," said Uncle Barnaby, "I know your dear, dead parents would sacrifice every cent of their darling children's inheritance for the sake of their precious children's health. But it won't come to that," he added more briskly. "The Wooden Nickel is my own ship, and you won't be eating any more aboard her than you would have here at home. She sails for Madagascar on tonight's evening tide, so you'll just have time to make it. You can eat your supper on the ship. Still—oh, the stress I shall be under, all the time you are away." He wiped his eyes once more before putting away his handkerchief.

In the same breath and almost the same words, Jane and Alan asked if they couldn't just run over and say good-bye to their friends the Pipers. But Uncle Barnaby shook his head. "No time."

Then, at last, Mr. Roderigo spoke up. "If we get to the ship fast enough, you can maybe write them a farewell postcard—"

"If you write real fast," said Captain Gonzorgo.

"—and we can mail it for you when we row back ashore for the rest of our crew."

"We'll even take care of the postage for you," Captain Gonzorgo added with a grin, as Mr. Roderigo put away his soggy handkerchief and got out a fresh one. (The thought passed through Alan's mind that Uncle Barnaby would have been much too economical to cry so much.)

So sister and brother were bustled away and aboard the Wooden Nickel almost before they were quite sure what was happening— pausing only to pick up a starfish Jane spotted writhing weakly above the tideline, and return it to the water on their way to the ship.

Once aboard, Captain Gonzorgo made Mr. Roderigo produce a postcard and pencil for Jane and Alan to write their hasty good-bye— saying not nearly all they wanted to tell Tom and Mary, because the whole family would be reading it, as well as Mrs. Moddle the Barnabyville Postmistress and Mr. Coddle the Barnabyville mail carrier.

Then Captain Gonzorgo and Crewman Roderigo got back in the ship's boat and returned to shore to mail the postcard and pick up the rest of their crew.

Was that why she married Uncle Barnaby? Because of only getting a quick postcard—signed by Jane and me both, to the whole Piper family?

No, because we found out later they never even got that postcard.

Then because she never had a real letter from me? But I would have written one, if I could have. And she says she only married my uncle to save me...

Here and now, Gonzorgo and Roderigo had begun their next step in his direction. Enough of a pause in the flash-past of Alan's life.

CHAPTER IV

What Alan knew about ships was that Uncle Barnaby owned six merchantmen, and that "to go astern" meant to go to the back, which was the end away from the figurehead. The figurehead on the Wooden Nickel had once been a wooden Indian outside a cigar store that Uncle Barnaby foreclosed on six months after the children came to live with him.[2] What Jane knew about ships was that they had "starboard" and "larboard" sides—though she never could remember which was which.

"But doesn't it seem odd," she asked, "that all the crew went ashore and has to be brought back two by two? How big a crew does the Wooden Nickel have, anyway?"

"What interests me right now," said Alan, "is where that supper is that Uncle Barnaby promised we could eat on the ship."

"Maybe," said Jane, "I'm supposed to cook it. I wish I knew for how many."

"Us, Captain Gonzorgo, Mr. Roderigo, and—say—at least two more crewmen. Start with supper for six, and if any others come, they'll have to get their own. There must be someone to cook for them when you aren't here—another member of the crew, I should think—and you're supposed to be an invalid, anyway. Out on a sea cruise for your health."

"So are you. But I can cook a lot better than you," Jane said proudly. "I paid attention to Uncle Barnaby in the kitchen. The 'gallery'[3] is what they call it on ships, isn't it?"

---

2   Apologies for what we nowadays recognize as a delicate allusion, but both wooden cigar-store Indians and Indian-head coins were hard historical facts of nineteenth-century American life, and can still be seen in some museums and antique shops.

3   She means "galley," not "gallery." Jane and Alan probably know even less about ships than Sir Joseph Porter did.

"I think so. Gallery, just like for pictures. And while you're finding that, I can look for stationery and pens to write real letters home."

"But how can we mail them?"

"Pass 'em to ships we meet sailing in the other direction. I think that's how sailors' letters always get home." Sometimes months and even years after being written—they might beat their own letters home—but he didn't mention that to Jane.

She said, "Oh, I see. I hope Captain Gonzorgo and Mr. Roderigo get back with the rest of the crew before those clouds reach us."

He squinted at them, like a mountain range on the horizon. "Has to be all right. They're seamen, after all, and have to know about these things."

They lit lamps in the gathering gloom, and Jane went below, where they reasoned the gallery should be, while Alan looked for the Captain's living room, where he thought he'd most likely find a writing-desk with stationery and pens. Should be somewhere up here on top, shouldn't it? And have a door near the foredeck or pupdeck or whatever they were called.

He had just found it, when Jane came rushing up, and this time she looked pale even to a brother's eyes, and even in the bad light. "Oh, Alan! Alan! Rats have chewed a lot of great holes down there, and the water's simply gushing in!"

"What? No wonder we're tilting! Or listing, or leaning, or whatever they call it when ships do it. And all Uncle Barnaby's trade goods will be lost!"

"And oh, where are Captain Gonzorgo and Mr. Roderigo? Shouldn't they have been back by now? It's getting blacker than the monstrous crow—the storm's right on top of us!"

He followed her out and down, saw with a glance that the hole or hold or whatever they called the place below the deck where they stored cargo and stuff was already too full of water for them to save any of the crates—there must be far too many rat holes to plug, even if they could swim down and find them and stay underwater long enough.

"Oh, Alan, what'll we do?"

"Find a lifeboat."

"Captain Gonzorgo and Mr. Roderigo took it!"

"There should be another one—I think ships always have two or three lifeboats."

But the Wooden Nickel didn't—not that they could find, anyway. Not with the rain and wind knocking the ship every which way. The storm had broken, with blinding flashes of lightning and deafening crashes of thunder, and rain sluicing down like huge cleavers of sharp water, and it was all Alan could do to keep tight hold of his sister by one hand...

In all that wind and rain, they hardly knew when the seawater broke over them and their feet weren't on deck any longer... because the ship sank, or maybe they got washed overboard first... here was a big loose log or stick—part of a broken mast, maybe—floating by for them to catch hold of, clutching and clinging for very life.

If it hadn't been for the storm, maybe Alan would have started suspecting a lot sooner. Suspecting that maybe it hadn't been rats that made those holes. That maybe all those crates that looked like they were filled with valuable trade goods were really empty, or else full of rubbish. That maybe there really was only one lifeboat—the one Gonzorgo and Roderigo had taken—and that they had left never intending to come back at all. That maybe they weren't even real seamen.

That maybe Jane never would have found any food to cook for supper.

Even if they had suspected any of that, they probably wouldn't have suspected Uncle Barnaby. They'd probably have thought it was a plot against him, too.

But how could anyone have made the storm come up like that, just when their plot needed it?

Only here, in the Toyland prison cell, as the soles of Gonzorgo's and Roderigo's back feet left the ground, did Alan wonder if anyone could be shrewd enough to wait and watch and not set their plot in motion until the weather conditions were such that a storm would almost certainly be coming up in a few hours.

CHAPTER V

What happened next was like a dream even in the flash-past of Alan's life.

It seemed that as they sank, the starfish they had rescued from the fast-drying sands swam up and revealed himself as a merman, or the king of all the starfishes, or the starfish king who became a merman in his own proper depth... it was confused. Whatever the case, he called his mer-court and they made a great bubble-dome of air around the two young land people.

It wasn't at all clear how long Jane and Alan spent there, dreamily watching mermaids and mermen swim-dancing lovely slow acrobatics all around their dome of underwater air. But, eventually, the Starfish King and his people carried their human visitors back up to the surface and put them ashore, where some friendly Gypsies found them and rearranged their own wanderings so as to bring the sister and brother within a stroll of home.

Their clothes were in tatters from the shipwreck. The kind Gypsies gave them some spare clothing. Because nobody outside the Piper household had ever seemed willing to befriend Uncle Barnaby's niece and nephew, they decided to go home disguised. Jane dressed as a boy and called herself Zindelo, the wolf of the wildwood, while Alan put on the clothes of a pretty young woman and called himself Floretta, the fawn of the forest. He made, if he did say so himself, a pretty fair (if dusky) Gypsy maid.

Besides spare clothing, the Gypsies gave Jane a lot of new recipes and Alan a lot of good tips for telling fortunes from cards, tea leaves, and people's palms. It turned out, you didn't need to know much at all about cards, tea leaves, or people's palms, if you used your wits, could figure out the people themselves, and told them whatever they most wanted to hear. They'd pay best and most happily for good news about their future, and if it turned out right, they'd remember you for a marvel. Otherwise, they'd likely as not have forgotten all about it by the time it turned out you'd been wrong. But if along with the prophecy you worked in some sound advice, you might just help make your good prophecies come true.

The Gypsy band brought them as far as Bunberry, where one turn in the road led to Toyland and the other to Spider Forest. No one went into Spider Forest unless they either absolutely had to, or knew a shortcut through there to someplace else, that could be done by daylight and would save them a very long way around. And there were strange tales about Toyland. So the Gitano (which was another word for Gypsies) followed the road straight on down to Barnabyville.

They encountered the villagers pouring out of Widow Piper's yard—almost everyone who lived in Barnabyville except the Piper children. It took no fortunetelling skills to learn what had happened— the villagers told it all soon enough. When Mr. Barnaby's niece and nephew were lost and presumed drowned at sea, he tried to make the people of the village he pretty well owned a little fonder of him by giving them a big party in Mrs. Piper's fields. Almost everyone came—except the Piper clan and their maid Hilda—and when the other villagers found out it was Mr. Barnaby throwing the party, and not Mrs. Piper, they all left in a body, wishing they dared hold poor Uncle Barnaby under the town pump.

They stopped (still munching refreshments from the party table) to have their fortunes read and watch the Gypsies dance, and no one recognized Alan or Jane. Villagers who half-grudged Mr. Barnaby's nephew Alan the time of day, besieged Floretta the fawn of the forest to have their palms read (and were very much impressed with Floretta's insights, Alan knowing more about them than they probably ever guessed). While he was busy with them, and those who were not waiting to hear their fortunes were applauding the Gitano dancers, Jane-as-Zindelo slipped on up to the Piper house.

When Floretta the fawn of the forest worked her way free and got up to join Zindelo, she had already revealed herself to Hilda Dolittle as Mr. Barnaby's niece, learned that Tom and Mary, not believing their sweethearts could really be drowned (especially since their Uncle Barnaby was the one who brought the tearful news), had set out to search the wide world for them, and that all of them—Tom and Mary and their brothers and sisters—were in danger of being step-fathered.

For one happy heartbeat, Alan thought the man might be Uncle

Barnaby, but even before he could ask, Hilda explained that rich Mrs. Piper's two suitors were Gonzorgo and Roderigo.

Jane exclaimed, "So they didn't drown, after all!"

"We were afraid they might have," Alan told Hilda. "And maybe two more crewmen as well, if they were caught in that little boat when the storm hit."

"Oh, no," Hilda said with a sigh. "More's the pity. For the last two years, ever since Mr. Piper died, Mrs. Piper has said that next time she'll marry only for love. And how she or anybody else could ever love either of those two, I'll never know! But come along, and we'll find some of Mary's clothes, or maybe Jill's, to fit Jane. Alan, you can probably put on something from Tom's or Jack's closet."

"Would you have known it was me, Hilda?"

"Oh, never, if I hadn't been told." But Hilda winked as she said it. Still, since all the villagers had seemed to be fooled, Alan hoped he might really have fooled Hilda, too, even if she was much more used to seeing him around than the rest of the village was.

He was about to follow her and Jane around to the kitchen door, when Mrs. Piper herself came out the front door. She took one look, clapped her hands, and cried, "Are you a real Gitano?"

"I am Floretta, the fawn of the forest," he replied in Floretta's gentle falsetto. "I peek into the future at two pennies the peek, collected in advance."

Mrs. Piper smiled, dug into her purse, and held out two shiny new pennies on her palm. "There. Peek for me."

He pocketed the pennies and pretended to study her palm. "Your name is Piper... Louisa Piper, born Jellicoe. You married a carpenter... named Carl... but he ceased to carp a little more than two years ago." Long enough that his widow and children remembered him lovingly but no longer tearfully.

"Yes. Poor Carl! Can my palm tell you how he died?"

"For a carpenter, it was an appropriate finish. A log fell on him." The joke wasn't Alan's. It had originated with Mary.

"Wonderful! You can really see all that in my palm?"

"And more. You have seven sons and seven daughters. The oldest daughter is named... Mary. She should marry a young man whose name begins with 'A.' He is charming, gifted, and handsome—everything that a young man should be, and a little more. To a lovely character he adds a shrewd sense of business—"

"Stop right there!" said Mrs. Piper. "If you're talking about that wretched, pitiful Alan Flinders who learned everything he knows about business from his shrewd Uncle Barnaby, you're quite wrong about him and my daughter."

Alan was stunned. Was this what Mrs. Piper really thought about him, after all those years of letting him and Jane play with her own children, and having them to lunch and dinner and an occasional slumber party, and all? But he cleared his throat, gentled his voice to Floretta's again, and amended his statement. "On closer inspection, his name begins with 'D.' Drew? Possibly 'Andrew'—yes, that accounts for the confusion."

"Very comfortably. Now, if you saw a 'B' there..." Mrs. Piper smiled and nodded in a way that made him wonder, just for a minute that day (though he clutched to it faster now, in the Toyland cell, than he and Jane had clung to that piece of wood when their uncle's ship went down), if she had recognized him after all, and only teased him with "wretched" and "pitiful."

Meanwhile, Captain Gonzorgo and Crewman Roderigo had come up to the Piper house and begun gushing praises onto Widow Piper until Alan thought she might drown in them.

"You have two suitors." Floretta made believe to see it in Mrs. Piper's palm. Just enough early suspicion was beginning to stir in his breast—not of Uncle Barnaby, but of the two supposed seamen—that he wondered which they were after, the widow or her money.

"Which shall I marry?" she asked Floretta... and from something in her voice, he thought she might wonder, too, whether they were really just fortune-hunters.

Floretta said, "I must read their palms first."

"A real Gypsy, are you?" said Gonzorgo. "Pretty one!"

"I am Floretta, the fawn of the forest. For two pennies—cash down, in advance—I read anyone's palm."

"You shall read mine first," said Gonzorgo. And bending close (and a little up, because he was a short man) he murmured at Floretta's ear, "Bid her wed me, and not just pennies, but diamonds and pearls shall be yours, fair one."

Hmmm, thought Alan. Tell them what they most want to hear... and I don't think Mrs. Piper really wants to hear she should marry either one of them. So what he finally said, scrutinizing Gonzorgo's hand, was, "I see a beautiful wife waiting for this handsome husband at home with patience... and a rolling pin in her right hand."[4]

Gonzorgo jerked and said, "What?" But Floretta held tight with his left hand and traced his right pointer finger mystically over his mark's palm as if its lines really showed him what he was talking about.

"Go on," said Mrs. Piper.

"The children are all asleep..."

"Whose children?" Gonzorgo and Mrs. Piper asked in almost the same breath.

"His," said Floretta. "He already has a wife, a blonde wife named Elizabeth, and nine rosy children."

"Not a word of truth!" cried Gonzorgo. "If you were a man—"

"I'm a sweet Gypsy maid," the fawn of the forest replied, standing closer to the widow. "And when it comes to scoundrels like you, we women have to stick together."

"Louisa—" Gonzorgo appealed to Mrs. Piper.

"Go!" She shooed him away. He scowled and retreated into the background.

Roderigo stepped into his place at once, beaming broadly. "Louisa, my sweet Louisa—"

"Stop!" the widow told the big man. "First let Floretta read your palm, too!"

"Fair is fair," Floretta remarked, holding out her hand.

Roderigo's smile faded, but he gave his two pennies to the Gypsy fortuneteller. "What you'll read there," he told her, "is that I'm so tender-hearted it really pains me to kill time."

"It does, indeed," Floretta agreed, studying his palm. "So much, that you never kill it at all. Instead, you spend it calling on a different girl every evening. Ooo, you naughty flirt, you!"

"I've heard enough," said Mrs. Piper, sounding very relieved. "Take yourselves off, both of you. I never want to see either of you again. But as for you, dear Floretta the fawn of the forest—for unmasking these rascals, may the blessing of a lonely widow follow you through life!"

"And never catch up!" Gonzorgo flung back even as he and Roderigo retreated.

And now the laws of Toyland had given them the upper hand.

4   In those days, an angry wife bashing her husband with her rolling pin was very popular image.

Alan was at their mercy, and they were another step closer to him. He could only pray they had never guessed who Floretta the fawn of the forest really was.

Suppressing a shudder, he took refuge in what remained of the flash-past of his life. While he still could.

CHAPTER VI

Jill all but forced Jane to borrow her best frock. Tom's clothes were a little too big for Alan, and Jack's a little too small. He opted for a little too big, even though Tom wasn't there to personally lend him a suit, and Jack was.

Dressed once again in garments of the right gender, they hurried home and burst in at the door, ready to give Uncle Barnaby a glad surprise.

At least, they thought so at the time. Not until yesterday had Alan considered—but he wasn't ready for yesterday to flash past, only to relive how happy he and Jane were, bursting in that day on Uncle Barnaby where he sat in his best frayed, half-sprung imitation horse-hair armchair in the uncarpeted living room.

"Uncle!" shouted Alan, and Jane—"Oh, Unkey, Unkey!"

Uncle Barnaby looked up and his jaw dropped as far as it could safely go. With overjoyed astonishment, they thought.

"Here we are, Uncle Barnaby!" Alan cried heartily. "Safe and sound!"

"And aren't you relieved and glad to see us again, Unkey?" added Jane.

"Relieved? Glad?" Uncle Barnaby murmured in what they took for happy shock. "Those are not the words."

"Not for us, either!" laughed Jane. "Too weak by half! Oh, Unkey—there just aren't any words for how happy we are to be home! Hasn't your heart just been breaking for us?"

"I have some... good enough glue."

Now Alan laughed. "Good one, Uncle Barnaby! The most expensive glue in the world couldn't mend a broken heart, and you'd never squander good money on the most expensive! But cheer up—you'll never be lonely again! That's the thought that kept us going, that brought us back home to you."

"Where we'll stay with you always," said Jane, "because we know what life would be to you without us."

Uncle Barnaby said, "You can't imagine."

"We're good and healthy now, all right," said Alan. "Thanks to all we've been through. And we won't go away again for our health unless you come along, too."

"Because we'll never leave you again," Jane promised. "Never!"

Their uncle said weakly, "Oh, joy."

"Until we're married, of course," Jane went on. "And then we'll settle down as neighbors."

"With the money we have from Mother and Father," said Alan. "We can wait for it till then."

Uncle Barnaby gave himself a shake. "I've taken good care of your money, never fear." He gave them a look that Alan only now saw had been more sharp than loving and concerned. "Who do you plan to marry, and when?"

"Tom Piper," Jane answered with a sigh. "Oh, dear Tom! If only he'd waited at home..."

"Mary for me," Alan boasted. "Dear, Contrary Mary!"

Uncle Barnaby made a strangled noise. Thinking he might have choked, Alan leaned over and slapped him on the back.

"Don't worry, Unk," said Alan, "maybe you can marry Mrs. Piper." He'd wondered about Uncle Barnaby spending all that money on an expensive party, but maybe love for the Widow Piper was what made him do it? Good thing Alan had gotten rid of his rivals Gonzorgo and Roderigo for him. "Now," he went on, "should we all go together and look for them, or would it be better to wait here where they'll be sure to find us when they come back?"

Uncle Barnaby said in a hoarse voice, "They've been sighted. In... in Toyland."

"Toyland!" cried Jane.

And Alan: "Who sighted them?"

"My... business associate there. Yes. Mr. Horner of Barnaby's Bodacious Bundles, the Toyland branch."

"Let's start right now!" said Alan. "We still have a few hours of daylight."

"We can sleep at Bunberry, and be in Toyland by lunchtime," said Jane.

Uncle Barnaby smiled at last. "You can be there a lot sooner than that."

"Travel by moonlight, you mean," Alan said eagerly, "and be there before breakfast? Yes—we won't get much sleep tonight anyway, thinking about Mary and Tom, and love will wing our heels all the way!"

"Why travel by moonlight?" Again Uncle Barnaby smiled. "Take the shortcut through Spider Forest."

"We've never been in Spider Forest," Jane said uneasily.

Alan was glad she was the one who raised the objection. It was easier for girls[5] to admit such doubts and misgivings, than it was for boys. To hearten her (and himself), he held her hand.

"Captain Gonzorgo and Mr. Roderigo know a shortcut to the shortcut through Spider Forest. They can go with you—they've got nothing else to do, now their ship has gone down."

"Yes," said Alan. "With all its crates of your trade goods. We're really sorry about that, Uncle."

Jane said, "but we're safe, anyway, and we're all together again, and that's the really important thing, after all. Isn't it, Uncle Barnaby?"

"Oh, yes. Yes, of course. That's the really important thing." Uncle Barnaby stood up. "I'll go find Captain Gonzorgo and Mr. Roderigo and send them back for you right away, so you can get started at once."

Alan almost remarked, because Mr. Roderigo is too tender-hearted to kill time. But it was Floretta who had heard that. Not a good idea to risk Roderigo and Gonzorgo figuring out that the fawn of the forest was Alan and vice versa.

Besides, Jane was saying, "But you're coming too, aren't you?"

"The Widow Piper will want to go as well. Likely bringing her whole brood, maidservant and all. After alerting them, I will join their party and meet you in Toyland. You hurry on ahead the fastest way,

5   I am aware that in my own generation, many fellow feminists began objecting to the use of "girls" for anyone older than about ten. In the era of this story, no one seems to have complained about it. Nor do I, not so long as grown and even elderly men are sometimes called "boys." I myself should prefer being called "old girl," if done in the same friendly tones used far too often to address me as "young lady"— which I find an insult, no matter how kindly meant, because it cannot help but be both hypocritical and dismissive of a lifetime's experience.

through Spider Forest with my captain and his man, to find Mary and Tom as quickly as possible, so that they don't slip away from us again before knowing you two are back safe and sound."

It made sense. A lot of sense at the time. Even more sense now, as Alan looked back on it. And very clever of Uncle Barnaby to cover up the fact that he intended to make Mary his own bride.

And now he had. She said she'd only done it to save him, Alan. But he was going to die anyway.

Gonzorgo and Roderigo were still only a step into the Toyland jail cell, and now Alan noticed that Roderigo had his handkerchief up to his eyes again.

CHAPTER VII

Roderigo had his handkerchief up to his eyes at the edge of Spider Forest, where he stood pointing down one-handed at a bird's nest on the ground.

"It's tumbled out of its tree," Roderigo sobbed. "And now the poor little birdie doesn't have a home anymore!"

"If you had a pump and some pipes," Gonzorgo told him, "you'd be a wonderful water works."

"Zorgey, have you no heart?"

"Locked in ice," Gonzorgo snapped. Then, glancing at Jane and Alan, "Where my heart has to be until we get through Spider Forest."

Alan was wondering at Mr. Roderigo's liberty in addressing the other as "Zorgey." Now that they had lost their ship, were they no longer captain and crew?

"But think of the poor little birdie," Roderigo burbled on, "without a home to lay its egg."

Alan stooped, picked the bird's nest up, and wedged it carefully into the highest fork he could reach of the overhanging tree. Roderigo thanked him tearfully on behalf of the poor little birdie, and put his handkerchief away until next time (which would probably be in about ten minutes).

Jane said, "Why do they call it Spider Forest? I've always wondered."

"And is it for one spider," said Alan, "or a whole horde of them?"

"A horde," said Roderigo.

"No, just one," said Gonzorgo. "The way I've heard tell. But a great, big one."

"Oh, dear!" Jane hesitated. "Maybe we'd better go around the long way, after all."

"What?" said Gonzorgo. "And take till tomorrow afternoon, when you could be there in an hour? Come on, and don't be silly. Chances are the great, big little spider is fast asleep somewhere far away from the shortcut, and we won't even see him."

"Oh, I hope we don't!" Roderigo sniffled.

"No," said Gonzorgo. "Still, it's a pity. He'd be something to see. A real tourist trap. Well, come on!"

Looking at Roderigo, Alan thought it must be nice, when you were a man, to be so big and strong and—obviously—courageous, that you felt free to cry whenever you liked. Which, with big Roderigo, was quite a lot of the time. But to be fair, Roderigo never seemed to cry because he was afraid of anything, just because he was tenderhearted and sentimental.

"Have you been in Toyland very often?" Alan asked the two men.

Both at once, Roderigo said "No" and Gonzorgo said "Often."

They paused, looked at each other, and Gonzorgo amended it to, "Once or twice. Nice enough place to visit."

"But you wouldn't want to live there?" said Alan. "Why not?"

"Well," Gonzorgo replied, "I never said quite that..."

"Cruel laws," Roderigo protested. "They have cruel laws."

"Not so much the laws," Gonzorgo said thoughtfully, "as the penalties and punishments for breaking 'em." He smacked his lips. "So you're safe enough so long as you never break any laws, and I can see where, yes, get on the buttered side of the bread, and it might not be the worst place in the world to settle down."

Jane remarked, "Because the name sounds like such a nice, friendly place... Toyland."

"What kind of laws?" Alan wanted to know.

"Well, for one," Gonzorgo told them, "nobody can make or sell any other toys than those that come straight out of the Master Toymaker's shop. He has very strict laws about that, does the Master Toymaker. Patents, copyrights, and local ordinances."

"What about Barnaby's Bodacious Bundles?" said Jane. "The main branch in Barnabyville has toys for sale."

"The branch in Toyland doesn't," said Gonzorgo. "That and any other store the Mayor lets do business in Toyland, does it only in non-toy items."

"Who is the Mayor of Toyland?" Alan asked.

Gonzorgo said, "The Master Toymaker."

"Oh," said Jane. "Like Uncle Barnaby is Mayor of Barnabyville."

"Yes, but even more so," the small man replied. "The Master directs it all, has his thumb in pretty well everything. One of his edicts requires every grown-up in town to visit his toyshop at least once a week—parents of small children, three times a week. That's every week except in December, when it's everybody's obligation every day. Sundays included."

"Oh, my!" said Jane. "All the children there must have so many beautiful toys!"

Uncle Barnaby's store in Barnabyville never actually sold any of its toys. The villagers gave their children spools and rag dolls to play with. From Barnaby's Bodacious Bundles, the villagers bought only what they absolutely had to have and couldn't get anyplace else or make for themselves. Uncle Barnaby made most of his money exporting goods he had imported more cheaply from somewhere else, or got from his villagers as payment-in-kind of their rents.

Alan said, "The Master Toymaker sounds like a busy man."

Roderigo sighed. "Not one to kill time."

"And he does it all himself?"

Gonzorgo snorted. "Not likely. He has plenty of day-workers in his toyshop, a Chief Apprentice to supervise them, and woe be to anyone who slips up or gets careless." He smacked his lips again.

Roderigo said, "And the Toyland Courthouse is separate, down on the city square."

"That's where they hold trials and uphold the Toymaker's laws," Gonzorgo explained. "Handy to the scaffold where punishments are meted out in the city square."

Alan said, "The Master Toymaker is the Judge?"

"Only for really grave cases," said Gonzorgo. "Mostly the Master Toymaker delegates day-to-day lawkeeping and suchlike minor jobs to a bench of judges and the various departments of government. They all have their offices right there in the Courthouse—Passport Office, Marriage Bureau, Jail, and so on, each one with its own Chief of Staff and assorted underlings. I hear the positions of Head and Assistant Jailor-Executioner are still open."

"The last ones," the big man snuffled, "broke their hearts when they had to execute somebody."

"That was years ago," said the small man. "Toylanders know what's good for them. Though every ten or fifteen years or so they may need a little brush-up lesson."

Jane said, "Passport Office? Do you need a passport to get into

Toyland?"

"Not to get in," said Gonzorgo. "Anybody can get in, any time they like. Only to get out again."

"You seem to know a lot about it," Alan mused, "for only having been there once or twice."

"We're good tourists," said Roderigo. "We pay attention."

Gonzorgo added, "It's the business of the captain of a merchant vessel to keep himself informed. But here we are!"

It was a good thing Gonzorgo and Roderigo knew the way, because Alan could barely see his own feet, let alone the trail beneath them, and he could tell that Jane was equally baffled. Were they in a ravine? After being twilight just a minute ago, now it was already dark as night.

"Almost there," Gonzorgo added heartily.

"Almost to Toyland?" Jane asked.

"No," Gonzorgo explained, "almost to the main shortcut, the one we've just taken a preliminary shortcut to reach. It's just at the end of this little gulley. Keep straight on the same way you're going, and you'll be out on the broad trail in no time. And from there—just half an hour's stroll to the city gates of Toyland and your sweethearts."

Roderigo started sobbing again in the darkness. Maybe he'd just felt his foot come down on a beetle.

"But aren't you going to stay with us?" said Jane.

"What for?" Gonzorgo replied. "You won't have any trouble staying on the right path from here on, and we've got pressing business of our own."

Roderigo blubbered, "And you're not—babies anymore—you're—you're all grown up now!"

That was the last good-bye they had. Before Jane and Alan knew it, they were alone in as good as night, and even the sound of Roderigo's weeping had faded away to nothing.

"Oh, Alan!" Jane whispered. "What shall we do?"

"Keeping walking ahead, and think about Tom and Mary." Part of Alan wished he was still little enough to confess he was scared, but the rest of him squared his shoulders and concentrated on being strong for Jane.

CHAPTER VIII

It was no good. They finally found their way out of the ravine, but now night had fallen over everything, and soon Jane, too, fell—over a tree root, and twisted her ankle badly, the same one she'd twisted when the scaffolding collapsed under them while they were painting their house. The autumn foliage was still thick, but just enough moonlight filtered through that Alan managed to spy a dark shadow that might be the mouth of a cave where they could find shelter.

He supported his limping sister over to it. She shivered on his arm. "There's a spider's web across it!" she said as a ray of moonlight picked it out.

"Not that big a web, and Mr. Spider doesn't seem to be at home. In its way, it's a good sign—if a spider had time to spin a web here and then abandon it, that must mean there isn't any bigger animal back in that cave."

"But, oh, look! There's a little white moth caught in the web. Poor moth! Even if the spider's abandoned his web, the moth will die, trapped there."

"No, it won't." Gently, Alan broke the strands closest around the moth and set it free. As it fluttered away and up in the moonlight, Jane gave a small cry of pleasure.

"There it goes," Alan observed, watching it as long as he could. "Flying for dear life. If only we could fly—straight to Mary and Tom!"

Jane sighed. "If only we could. I surely can't walk any farther on this ankle. I hope you're right, about the spiderweb meaning no bears or wolves are at home in there. Or skunks or porcupines or things."

Alan finished the rest of the spiderweb off with one sweep of a dead stick, and they settled down in the mouth of the little cave... not quite daring to go farther back into the pitch darkness, but resting as comfortably as they could, Jane in the crook of her brother's arm.

"Toys for every child in Toyland," Jane said softly. "How wonderful must that be! Alan, do you suppose that's why none of the other children of Barnabyville would play with us, except the Pipers? Because we had toys from Uncle Barnaby's shop, and they thought we were stuck up about it?"

"I'd say they were the stuck-up ones—too proud to let us share with them. Except the Piper kids, of course."

"Maybe Mrs. Piper was the only one in Barnabyville who could afford real, store-bought toys for her children."

"We only got them when they were dusty from sitting on show. Remember how we used to wipe them off with a damp rag?"

"And do you remember that pretty little doll with a china head, that Jill and I played with a whole summer, until Simon tried to feed it blackberries, and when Jill washed it with soap and water, all the paint came off its face, and its little sawdust body fell apart?" Jill yawned.

Alan told her, "Try to get a little sleep."

"I wish I could, but I'm frightened."

"Don't be. Nothing's going to hurt us." Alan sincerely hoped he was right. "Darkness is nothing to be afraid of, because—because darkness is nothing at all. Just the absence of light."

"I can hear so many wood creatures rustling around us... Will they let us alone? They left the Babes in the Wood alone, only when the Babes in the Wood died, the birds came and covered them both up with leaves..."

Alan laughed—it came out sounding pretty fair. "Well, we aren't exactly the Babes in the Wood. We're all grown up. But the wood creatures will let us alone, because we're letting them alone. And we aren't going to die and have the birds cover us with leaves—we're going to wake up in the morning feeling refreshed and ready to find Tom and Mary. Now please, Jane, shut your eyes and let yourself drift off. Your big brother is right here beside you." Big brother tried not to wish he had Mother and Father and Uncle Barnaby, or even one of them, right there beside him.

Jane sighed again, and he thought she shut her eyes, by the way her head lolled down and, sooner than he might have expected, her breathing grew slow, gentle, and regular. Before he was quite aware of it, he drifted off, too...

Into dreaming... more dreams like those of the Starfish King, that even with his whole life flashing past his eyes, he couldn't be sure whether they were only dreams, or confused memories of things that might really have happened. This time it seemed as though the white moth was back, and she was the Moth Queen, a beautiful, motherly lady with great white wings. And the spider came back after all—a spider as big as a bear—but there was a real, actual bear (or at least a real, actual dream-bear) there, too, that fought the spider and killed it with a flaming cutlass until it—the spider—burned to ashes and the Moth Queen blew them away with a flutter of her wings, then clapped her hands and summoned her whole royal court of moths and butter-flies, who did a wonderful flying ballet that lasted into the morning twilight, when Alan woke up first, gently and in perfect safety, and a moment later his sister woke up and announced that her ankle felt good enough to walk on.

They were so hungry, they stuffed every berry they could find into their mouths, and tried to crack some nuts with fist-sized rocks. In their search for nuts and berries, they found the path that led them out of Spider Forest to within sight of the glistening gates of Toyland.

Toyland, where Gonzorgo and Roderigo had hurried ahead, to ap-ply for the Jailor-Executioners' vacant positions, while Jane and Alan thought they were doubling back to see to some pressing business in Barnabyville. But the flash-past hadn't reached the time when Alan found out about that.

CHAPTER IX

It had reached the first place they headed once they were in Toyland—the Christmas Tree Grove, a sort of town park so heavily wooded with pines and firs that it promised them a good place for resting while they planned their next move.

Not half a dozen steps inside the Grove, who should they find but Mary and Tom!

"Mary!"

"Alan!"

"Jane!"

"Tom!" all four of them calling one another's names at once.

"Tom, old fellow," Alan suggested, "don't you think now's a time when two's company and four is a town meeting?"

"Point taken, old man," cried Tom, linking Jane's eager arm through his and running off together with her. She had still been limping between Spider Forest and Toyland, but the sight of Tom must have finished untwisting her ankle completely.

Mary fell into Alan's arms. Catching her was the greatest joy of his life up to this moment.

When they finally stopped kissing, he said (still happily hugging her), "So Uncle Barnaby's information was right!"

"What information?"

"Mr. Horner, who manages the shop's Toyland branch, reported seeing you and Tom here in town."

Mary shook her head. "Oh, no! Oh, no! Hilda—who luckily met us before Mother or any of the others saw us—told us they had no idea we were here, but he—your Unkey Barnaby—" the sarcasm in Mary's imitation of Jane was, as usual, directed at Uncle Barnaby—"said as long as he had some kind of business proposition for the Master Toymaker, they might as well start looking for us in Toyland as anyplace else."

Now Alan shook his head, more in bafflement than denial. "No... Maybe he was keeping it back to surprise them... But he was afraid you and Tom might leave again before he could get here with your family. That's why he sent Jane and me on ahead by the shortcut."

Mary laughed. "You took the shortcut—and that's why they beat you here!" Then, "What shortcut?"

"The one through Spider Forest."

"Oh, Alan, Alan!" She hugged him tighter. "When will you ever wake up about your Uncle Barnaby?"

"But you're the one who should wake up, Mary!"

"Me and all the rest of Barnabyville? And you and Jane are the only ones who are right about him?"

"You'll especially be sorry for saying all these things about him, if he marries your mother and becomes your stepfather."

Mary drew back and stared at Alan. "What are you talking about? It's me your nasty old Uncle Barnaby wants to marry."

"You! Oh, no! No, you've got to be mistaken, Mary! You've got to be mistaken."

"I'm not mistaken," Mary said grimly. "He wants to marry me, get rid of all the rest of my family if he can—maybe by sending them on a long sea cruise in a leaky ship or a shortcut through Spider Forest—and have Father's money to hoard away with his own fortune, and yours and Jane's, too. Oh, Alan, Alan, don't you see the losing game your Uncle Barnaby is playing with you?"

"How... How long has Uncle Barnaby been wooing you?"

"Well, the first time he actually tried it in so many words, was the same day he came telling us you and Jane were lost at sea."

"Oh! Then he must have known he'd need someone to comfort him in his loneliness." But why Mary and not her mother? "He never said a word about it after we got back—only that you and Tom wouldn't take his word for our deaths and had hurried off searching for us."

"Searching for you, yes. Even if I hadn't wanted to get away from your Uncle Barnaby—as far and as fast as I could!—I'd still have come along with Tom to search for you and Jane."

"Then why stop here in Toyland—though I'm awfully glad and grateful that you did—and what is that costume your brother has on?"

Alan had had just had a quick glimpse of it, before Tom ran away with Jane. It looked like what Alan had seen in pictures and on a boy doll that once came through Barnaby's Bodacious Bundles. For some reason, when a woman wore servants' dress—like Hilda, if Hilda had ever once worn anything else but ordinary everyday clothing—it was called "maid's uniform," but when a man wore it, it was called "livery." Tom's looked richer than any clothes they had ever seen on real people in Barnabyville, servants or not, for any occasion. Even Uncle Barnaby, who could afford to buy fine garments but never did, and the Piper family, who could have afforded dressing up on occasion, if they had ever considered any occasions special enough to dress up for.

"It's court dress," Mary replied. "We were robbed on the road—"

"Robbed!"

"Yes. By two masked men, a small one waving a pistol around, and a big one holding a handkerchief to his eyes."

"Odd," Alan mused, wondering. In that couple of days between when Captain Gonzorgo and Mr. Roderigo got back to Barnabyville with news of the Wooden Nickel going down, and Jane and Alan getting home themselves after their time with the Starfish King and the Gypsies, could...? No. It had to be just coincidence.

Mary was going on, "Luckily, Tom found work as a Chief Factotum of the Court Toyal.[6] It's only for long enough to fill our pockets again so we can continue our search—"

"You don't need to continue your search," Alan reminded her lovingly. "Not now. What's a 'factotum'?"

"Like a servant-of-all-work, but the title makes it sound fancier and more impressive. We still need to get away from your Uncle Barnaby. We can go together—get lost in some trackless desert somewhere in the west, and settle down to enjoy our little spats, the way married people do..."

For some minutes, they lost themselves cozily in playing at the kinds of squabbles husbands and wives were always teased about having with each other. All the time smugly congratulating themselves that they, Mr. and Mrs. Alan Flinders, would be far too wise ever to squabble in real earnest about silly little things.

And now Mary was Mrs. Barnaby. Could it have been that business about the girl just teasing and pretending to hate the man she

6   "Toyal" could be a misprint for "Royal" in the libretto as published by Theatre Arts Press, © 2018. But I like it, and it seems fittingly consistent.

truly loved, all the way up the moment of saying, "I do"? Would she be playing at spats and squabbles with Uncle Barnaby, when Alan was gone?

Even after he told her all that he had finally found out...

But the flash-past wasn't there yet.

CHAPTER X

It was, however... not a quarrel, not really... No, you couldn't really call it a quarrel, not as such... but a heavy puzzle. Mary persisted in acting dead set against revealing her and Tom's presence in Toyland to Uncle Barnaby and even her own mother, since the Widow Piper had come with Uncle Barnaby. While Alan saw no reason not to announce right away that everybody was found. That was the whole reason they had all come here from Barnabyville, wasn't it? And surely—surely—Mary was mistaken about Uncle Barnaby wanting to marry her. She was contrary, after all—it was a lifelong habit with her, and usually it both looked good on her and served her pretty well, but this time... Or maybe she was right, so far as that went, except that Uncle Barnaby had just gone a little temporarily crazy at losing his niece and nephew, and that was over and done with, now he had them back safe.

But when Jane and Tom came back to the Christmas Tree Grove, bringing lunch for everyone—fried chicken, very sweet lemonade, taffy apples, and very very sweet cupcakes; a meal so sweet that Mary didn't even sugar her chicken—Tom sided with Mary. "Well... Jane and Alan could maybe join 'em, but only if they promised not to say a word about me and Mary being here."

"So we can wait for just the right moment," Mary said, more like a threat than a promise, "and surprise them then. But can you both keep it secret?" She looked at Alan and Jane.

"For you, Mary, I could even pepper my lemonade." Especially sweet as it was.

"I wish we could." Mary sighed. "Everything in Toyland is too sweet by more than half. But Tom forgot to bring his poor little sister any pepper."

"I wouldn't have forgotten the pepper," Tom replied, "if Jane had said she wanted it."

"Jane was right there with you."

"I hadn't tasted the lemonade yet," said Jane.

"But now," Tom went on, "I'd better be getting back to my job at the Toyland Courthouse, if we want this week's pay." Now he was the one who sighed. "It's hard work, pretending to be busy."

"Poor fellow!" Alan teased him, and Jane said, "Don't even pretend to clear up your own after-lunch mess, we'll do it for you."

Tom had hardly gotten out of the Grove before a stranger in frayed black velvet came in. With hardly a glance in the young people's direction, he sat down on an empty bench, heaved a heavy sigh, and buried his head in his arms, muttering something that sounded like, "What'll I do? What'll I do?"

Alan coughed. "Something the matter, sir?"

The stranger looked up at them. He had pepper-and-salt hair and a bright red neckerchief. "They've seized all my puppets! My show posters are up all over town, and the town officials have confiscated all Marmaduke's Life-Sized Marionettes. Oh, why did I ever come to Toyland?"

Mary said, "For the box-office receipts, perhaps?"

The stranger groaned.

"I wish we could help you," said Jane.

"Life-sized marionettes?" said Alan. "Say, maybe we can! Remember that little Irish melodrama we played last summer to celebrate painting the Barnabyville town pump?"

"Almost nobody came to see it," Mary pointed out, "besides the rest of the Piper family."

"But your brothers and sisters made us a lovely audience, almost all by themselves," said Jane. "And there were a few others who stayed."

"And you'd be Marmaduke?" Alan guessed, with another look at the stranger.

"Yes, I'm Delancey Marmaduke. Owner and puppeteer of Marmaduke's Life-Sized Marionettes. When I had them. But now they're gone—confiscated—my entire company!"

"Would you want to put strings on us?" Mary asked suspiciously, "and work us like marionettes?"

Marmaduke shook his head. "That's why they confiscated my marionettes—calling their strings a 'choking hazard.' But you could be clockwork automatons! I don't think Toyland has any laws outlawing clockwork automatons. Not yet."

Mary said, "There's a rumor going around Toyland that the Master Toymaker is about to demonstrate a whole parade of some new kind of big, marching toy soldiers. That sounds like they could be clockwork."

"Then we're just in time!" cried Delancey Marmaduke. "We can give our show right after the parade! And then use our box-office take to get out of Toyland before they have time to pass a law outlawing every other clockwork automaton except the Master Toymaker's."

"Us clockwork automatons might want to stay a little longer," said Alan. "What'd be our share of that box-office take?"

Marmaduke said, "How about a third?"

Uncle Barnaby's nephew thought about dickering for half or even two-thirds, seeing how desperate Mr. Marmaduke acted for their help. But a third seemed pretty fair. "All right," he agreed. "In advance."

"Even if I knew in advance what our take would be, I don't have the money to pay you until our audience has paid me to see you. You can have your share right before curtain time."

Mary wanted to know, "What shall we do for costumes?"

"And make-up?" Jane added.

"They didn't confiscate my marionettes' costume trunks, only the Life-Sized Marionettes themselves. Yes... yes, I think their costumes should fit you. And make-up, too—I use regular stage make-up on them, so I can wipe it off and change it for the different characters, depending on what play we do. You say you three already have a play? You can run it by me in my tent."

Marmaduke had set up his tent in the Toyland Town Park. "They didn't make any trouble about that," he explained, "when I applied for my permits and passport out of Toyland again. Only about my marionettes with their choking-hazard strings."

"We'll be good clockwork automatons," Alan promised, already practicing clockwork-looking movements.

"Did you put up this great tent all by yourself?" Mary asked, looking around. It had a ticket stand at the entrance and a curtained-off smaller tent behind for the dressing-room. But the main tent alone was at least as big as the Pipers' whole house, with benches on risers all around the central playing area.

"Wherever I go," Mr. Marmaduke told them, "I hire local roustabouts just to help me set up and break camp afterwards. Here, I hired

Toyland's two Jailor-Executioners. They're just newly appointed to their positions, and were looking to fill in their spare hours profitably. Toyland doesn't hold that many executions."

Jane said, "Tom's mentioned what hard work it is just looking busy when you don't really have anything to do."

Alan said, "You were able to pay them right away?"

"Well, no. They were willing to wait for their money."

Had Marmaduke given any description at all of Toyland's new Jailor-Executioners, Jane and Alan would surely have guessed who they were. That might have made Jane and Alan suspect... but what would they have done any differently than they did?

They found ideal costumes right away and got into them at once (the girls behind a dressing-screen): Mary as an Irish colleen, Jane as the Daughter of the Regiment, and Alan as some kind of officer in the same Regiment. They were slathering on their make-up—heavily, to hide the fact that they were real people—when who should duck in through the back flap but the next-to-oldest Piper girl—Mary's sister Jill. Followed by a pleasantly homely young fellow wearing spectacles and a worried frown.

"Mary!" cried Jill. "So here you are, you naughty Mary Piper!"

"And here I intend to stay, you nice Jill Piper. Or are you being naughty today, too?"

"And Jane and Alan!" Jill clapped her hands and giggled. "Tom never let on that you were here, too."

"What about Tom?" demanded Jane.

"Oh, he's right there at the Toyland Courthouse, doing his job, which seems to consist of waiting around for somebody to want him. Mama wanted him, but he just told her, 'I'm a big boy now, Mama. I'm earning my own money, I'm not going back with you, and I don't know where Mary is.' And here you are!" Jill clapped her hands again. "Oh, don't worry, Miss Contrary Piper—I guess I can keep a secret as well as my big brother can—but better put on plenty of make-up, so Mama and Old Barnaby and the others won't know you if they come to the show."

"Phoo!" Mary answered with a toss of her head. "I'm not worried about them. I'm grown up, too. Almost as old as Tom." But she slathered on a few more heavy layers of make-up.

Meanwhile, the bespectacled young man was looking closely at Alan's and Jane's costumes. "Those look just like the uniforms of the

Lifesize Clockwork Regiment!"

"Do they?" Mr. Marmaduke asked uneasily. "The Toymaker and I must both have seen that same opera poster. I hope Toyland doesn't have any laws about that?"

"I don't... think so. I think I'd know about something like that, being Chief Apprentice Toymaker."

"Apprentice to the Master Toymaker?" Mr. Marmaduke sounded more nervous than ever.

"Yes, and you can't be any more worried about it than I am. You see, I'm in charge of the parade today, and I... must've wound the Clockwork Captain too tight, or something, and now he won't go at all."

"So we're in a pickle here," said Jill. "The rest of the clockwork soldiers are ready to march, but they need their Captain to lead 'em. So Grumio thought, you being a puppet master, Mr. Marmaduke, and knowing all about Life-Sized Marionettes—"

"Which your people confiscated from me," said Mr. Marmaduke. "No, I can't help you."

"Wait a minute," said Alan. "Maybe I can! As long as I'm dressed for the part anyway, and wouldn't mind having the chance to practice being clockwork."

Mary said, "And a little extra publicity never hurts."

"That's right!" cried Jane. "Captain Clockwork, just lead everybody right back here to Mr. Marmaduke's tent after the big parade!"

Well, no, he couldn't have done that, exactly. There'd have been that much more chance that the Master Toymaker might notice the Clockwork Captain who led the parade wasn't the same Clockwork Captain who had left the toyshop.

Not that, in the long run, it would have made that much difference. Toyland's new Executioners would still have been about to earn their pay for what they had been hired to do.

CHAPTER XI

Marching like a clockwork automaton was easy enough. Standing still like one was not, posed right there in front of the reviewing stand, while Mayor Master Toymaker did his song and dance about what a wonderful city-state he ran and what a great thing he had done inventing this wonderful Clockwork Regiment to protect it from any and all future threats.

Uncle Barnaby had a seat near the reviewing stand, beside Widow Piper and her dozen younger children (including Jill, who naturally sat beside her twin Jack, but seemed to have eyes only for Chief Apprentice Toymaker Grumio at her other shoulder). None of them seemed to recognize Alan beneath his layers of make-up and his straight-ahead automaton stare, blinking as little as he could. It was hard not to blink during Mayor Master Toymaker's big speech.

The Master Toymaker went on and on, but it all seemed to boil down to: "My toys are Toyland's only export. They talk and walk and do everything but think. I can give them everything but a soul, and someday I may give them even that. This is a land you will never forget, a land you will dream of for all your years to come."

Then at last he led his people in their National Anthem, where he did the verses and directed the whole group in each chorus, including the Clockwork Regiment, since they were among his talking as well as walking toys:

> *Toymaster.* When you've grown up, my dears,
> And are as old as I,
> You'll often ponder on the years
> That roll so swiftly by,
> My dears,
> That roll so swiftly by.
> And of the many lands
> You will have journeyed through,

You'll oft recall the best of all:
The land your childhood knew!

All. Toyland! Toyland!
Little girl- and boy-land.
While you dwell in it,
You are ever happy then.
Childhood's joyland,
Mystic, merry Toyland!
Once you pass its borders
You can ne'er return again.

Toymaster. When you've grown up, my dears,
There comes a dreary day
When 'mid the locks of black appears
The first pale gleam of gray,
My dears,
The first pale gleam of gray.
Then of the past you'll dream,
As gray-haired grown-ups do,
And seek once more its phantom shore:
The land your childhood knew!

All. Toyland! Toyland!
Little girl- and boy-land.
While you dwell in it,
You are ever happy then.
Childhood's joyland,
Mystic, merry Toyland!
Once you pass its borders
You can ne'er return again.

Finally it was over. Grumio slipped down from the stands and pretended to start Alan's clockwork again so he could lead the Clockwork Regiment back. Once out of sight of the reviewing stand, Grumio brought back the real Clockwork Captain, who had apparently just needed a little rest from being overwound, and worked him into place, letting Alan get back to Mr. Marmaduke's tent in the Toyland Town Park. Mary and Jane were waiting, Jane patiently and Mary not.

Mary greeted Alan's appearance with the words, "Oh, isn't it cunning?"

"Somebody must have started its works," Jane joined the teasing, "and it ran away."

"And doesn't it seem natural?" Mary teased on.

Alan kissed her.

"Oh!" cried Jane (but she waited till he was done, for now, with his kissing), "it's alive!"

"Well, just now," said Alan, "but if we all work and study very, very hard, we may someday aspire to be good little clockwork automatons."

"Like toys from the Master Toymaker's shop," said Mary.

"The pinnacle of our aspirations! He makes them walk and talk and do everything but think," Alan parroted the Master Toymaker's mayoral speech. "Someday he may even give them souls!"

"Hurray for the Master Toymaker!" both girls laughed, not quite in unison. Then Mr. Marmaduke ducked in to say that the show tent was full of an audience waiting for the show they'd all paid to see.[7]

---

7   In our own hypersensitive era, this episode looks touchy. But Victor Herbert took lifelong patriotic pride in his Irish roots, "MacDonough" is a surname of Irish origin, and the Irish look like a preeminent example of a minority parlaying ridicule into popular acceptance. Humor remains prominent in our St. Patrick's Day celebrations, when "Everybody is Irish." I have drawn the Irish melodrama almost line for line from MacDonough's libretto, making only minor verbal changes and substituting a quatrain based on "The Night Paddy Murphy Died" (a ballad attributed to Johnny Burke, 1851-1930, of Newfoundland, but happily subsumed into the Irish folk tradition) for Irene Cassidy's quatrain in the libretto, which runs,

> Ah, dinna me deelish, the goolenn is dooleen.
> The agra is climbing the side of the bawn,
> Hurroo, and megoo. And avick for the colleen,
> Ah, dinna ma deelish, my heart it is tawn.

All this said, I must confess that none of this play-within-a-play sequence appears ever to have reached the Broadway stage. Apparently before opening night, itinerant puppetmaster Marmaduke had transmogrified into Inspector Marmaduke of the Toyland Police, with appropriate changes to the libretto. For various reasons, I (like James Howe before me) opted to keep the puppetmaster version.

Mary went into the show tent first. Centering her slender self in the playing area, she struck a tragic if mechanical-looking pose, head back with one arm thrown jerkily across her forehead, and declaimed: "Oh, wirrah, wirrah, 'tis a sad day for Imogene Cassidy! The village of Ballymagha is overrun with sassenachs."[8]

Alan's cue to stride in as the villain of the play. Still, naturally, in his uniform, originally copied from a poster for an Italian opera, now serving to identify him as an officer in the British army. In puppet theater, a uniform was a uniform.

The trickiest part was remembering to act stiff and a little jerky, like a clockwork automaton. At least, if he forgot a line, all he had to do was jerk and whirr until it came back. "Tell me, wench," he demanded in a mock-English accent as thick as her mock-Irish brogue, "what 'tis y' discuss so secretly with y'r own sweet self."

"Back, Captain Montmorency!" she answered, thrusting her arms out as if to hold him off. "Back! As far as iver ye can! An' occupy yon bench."

"I perceive here no bench."

"Nor be there niver any 'wench' hereabout."

"Aha! Me proud beauty, you defy meh!"

Flinging up her chin, Mary-as-automaton Irene Cassidy glared back at him and cried, "I do!"

"One more word, and I whistle for the British army and have you shot."

"Rinnygade! Shure an' begorrah, there's anither word for ye, an' what's more, a true ain."

Automaton Captain Montmorency whistled Jane's cue to appear in her Daughter of the Regiment uniform, bearing her prop musket.

"Army," he ordered her, "shoot yonder fair colleen."

Carefully wearing no expression at all, the British army lifted its musket to its shoulder and took aim.

"Stop!" the colleen countermanded.

"You crave, perhaps, a moment to pray?" inquired Captain Montmorency.

"'Nay, 'tis nae that—but Imogene Cassidy be an Irish heroine, an' canna die wi'out a song." Shaking her bobbed brown curls, she cleared her throat and warbled off soulfully:

---

8   wirrah = worry; sassenachs = Saxons (here, the English).

Oh, the night that Paddy Murphy died, Oi never can forgit!
We all got roarin' drunk that night, an' some ain't sober yit.
But th' only thing we did that night that fills me heart wi'
    fear—
We tuke th' ice right off the corpse an' put it in the beer.

Her warm Irish sentiment melted the cold British hearts. Musket wavering, the army looked at its officer. He, with his handkerchief at his eyes (thinking of Roderigo), shook his head, an utterly reformed villain. "The British army cannot shoot a voice like yours. Sing again, my fair colleen—sing happier songs—and let us all, each and every, join you in the chorus."

The rest was easy, as the three mock automatons led their audience in a rousing singalong of as many ditties as they could think of to fill an hour's entertainment and send everyone away still whistling and humming.

How many of yesterday's audience would be the same people gathering out there today in the Toyland town square to watch his execution?

CHAPTER XII

Mr. Marmaduke's feet were hardly touching the ground when he re-entered the dressing-tent. "Don't take anything off yet, my dear, dear clockwork marionettes! His Honor the Master Toymaker himself has engaged us for a private performance tonight!"

"This would be the same His Honor," Mary said suspiciously, "who had your property confiscated this morning?"

Mr. Marmaduke waved his hand. "That was his minor town officials, over-interpreting a law already on the books, about marionette strings as choking hazards. His Honor the Mayor is, personally, very much impressed with what he saw this afternoon. Play it right tonight, and we stand to add a nice, tidy little sum to our afternoon's profits. Maybe even get my real marionettes back this side of the town gates."

Mary said, "Are we your 'unreal' marionettes, then?"

As if he hadn't even heard her, Mr. Marmaduke went on, "What a show we might work up with you and them together! Me pulling their strings while you three interact with your clockwork routine..."

"Are we going up to the castle?" Jane asked eagerly. As castles went (never having seen any outside of picture books, Alan couldn't be sure), the Toymaker's castle might itself be like a toy; but it was still an impressive abode, twice as big as the Pipers' house, with a six-foot wall encircling it and four little turrets poking their heads up above the main roof, like an elephant lying on its back with its legs up in the air. (They'd also only ever seen elephants in picture books.) It looked very pretty and picturesque sitting there on its little hill on the edge of town.

But Mr. Marmaduke said, "No, we're to go to his toyshop here in town. He plans to be working late this evening."

Alan asked, "Will we have to keep up our clockwork act the whole way there?"

"I'll take my little yellow caravan wagon, and you can ride enclosed in back, have a little rest and maybe a bite to eat along the way."

The twilight was pretty deep by now, this time of year, and Mr. Marmaduke not all that familiar with the layout of Toyland, so Grumio rode up front with him, while the three mock automatons had their quick bite in back, safe from anyone's view. The puppeteer's rye bread rolls, sausage, and cold unsweetened tea tasted very good after the Toyland fare.

"I wish we could get a sausage and a roll over to Tom," said Jane. "Is the Courthouse open so late?"

"No," Mary replied, "but Tom has a little bedroom in back, where he can answer the night bell if anyone rings it."

"Do we pass the Courthouse?" said Jane.

Alan answered, "It's where the Toymaker gave his speech today as Mayor of Toyland. That's right—you were back in Mr. Marmaduke's tents with Mary. You didn't miss much."

Mary, who had lived in Toyland for a week with her brother, said, "The Courthouse is right across the town square from the Toymaker's shop, which is every bit as big and twice as important. But just now we can't let anybody see us as anything else than clockwork automatons, so going outside the wagon even long enough to take Tom a sausage is definitely out."

"Your whole family was there for the show today," said Jane.

"Along with your Uncle Barnaby." Mary made a face.

"Did any of them recognize us? Besides Jill, who already knew."

"A few of them may have, but if they tried to say anything, Jill would have headed 'em off."

The wagon came to a stop. After a moment, Mr. Marmaduke opened its door and whispered to its three passengers, "Remember; no one but me knows how to start or stop you. That's what I told the Master Toymaker."

Well, Grumio had made believe to start and stop Alan, but that was when he was filling in for the Captain of the Clockwork Regiment. Now, even though the coast looked clear and the alley was pretty dark in the gathering gloom, lit only by the toyshop's curtained back windows, Alan, Mary, and Jane adopted their mock clockwork march, whirring a little in their throats as they stiff-stepped from the wagon into the building.

They entered a long, shadowy room that smelled of cats and

clean dust. Cats because everybody had them, to keep down the rats and mice; dust because the Master Toymaker apparently didn't hire enough help to keep his back room well cleaned, once his toys were turned out and the rest of the workers gone home. Most of what light seeped in came from the back door on the alley, which was not quite so dark yet as inside the building; and there was just enough of it to see floor-to-ceiling shelves lining the walls everywhere except where there were doors: one at the far end and one midway. Quite a lot of the Clockwork Regiment was lined up at attention, every soldier touching all the others close to him, all along the walls, in front of the shelves.

Grumio shut the alley door behind them, lit a lantern, and looked around. Nobody else was in the long, shelved room, just the five of them. And about half the soldiers of the Clockwork Regiment. "This is the storeroom," the Toymaker's Apprentice told the others in a low voice. "I guess you can relax a minute. He must be waiting in his office." Grumio pointed to the door at the far end. Then, shining his lantern at the door midway (which was harder to see because of the shelves): "Here's the hallway that goes to the showroom where we sell our toys, nine to five every day except during December, when it's six to nine. Only it was closed all day today for the Parade and Presentation of the Clockwork Regiment."

"I thought he presented them all to the town?" said Mary.

"He did, but we're still storing them here until the town can build a special new barracks for them. And the workroom where we make the toys is right across the hall. Better take your positions now, and be ready to freeze."

Grumio went to the door of the Master Toymaker's office, knocked, waited a minute, knocked again, waited again, and called softly, "Master?" At last, still getting no answer, he opened the office door and peered in.

"Not there," he announced, stepping back out. "But he has to be expecting you, or he wouldn't have left his little lamp lighted in there. He must have stepped over to the necessary,[9] or maybe he's in the workroom."

The apprentice went out the hallway door, and Mary said, "I guess it'd be all right to have a seat on these benches here. After all, we're good little joint-limbed automatons, who might as well be sitting as standing."

9   In this era, the "necessary" was often an outhouse.

"I don't see why you shouldn't," said Mr. Marmaduke. "I'll see if I can find another lantern or lamp in the Master Toymaker's office." He headed there.

They settled themselves, largely by feel, on the nearest bench and gazed around in the gloom. "Not a bad warehouse," Alan decided. "Though I wonder why they don't have all the toys boxed, to save them from getting dusty?"

"And almost all of them seem to be dolls," Mary observed. "Big dolls, little dolls—and character dolls, pretty well all of them. I wonder if there are stuffed animals and tops and blocks and things on the lower shelves, where the clockwork soldiers hide 'em from view."

"Oh!" Jane exclaimed. "That doll winked at me!"

Mary scooped a cat away from her leg and said, "This place is too spookylarious by half."

"We could just run for it," Alan remarked, looking back at another of the Toymaker's cats, which was peeping out to inspect him. "If we weren't getting our cut for helping Mr. Marmaduke."

"Heard that," said the puppeteer, coming back with a lighted candle. "Thanks for sticking around."

"Shhh!" said Jane. "They're coming."

The three mock marionettes went carefully stiff and glassy-eyed as the Master Toymaker came in, with Grumio tagging at a respectful distance behind him.

Mr. Marmaduke bowed. "Your Honor. Here I am, ready to repeat my moral and amusing entertainment at your command." He coughed apologetically. "Might I request... my payment in advance? Their machinery is very delicate."

"And very marvelous," came the Master Toymaker's mellifluous voice. "As I witnessed this afternoon. Your own handiwork?"

"Entirely." Mr. Marmaduke coughed again. Though Alan couldn't have seen it without turning his head, he could picture the puppeteer holding out one hand in a manner Uncle Barnaby would have approved.

"My office," said the Toymaker, "is the proper place to conclude our business. Come. You also, Grumio."

The Master Toymaker led the other two into his office and shut the door behind them, leaving Alan, Jane, and Mary... not quite in total darkness, but in not enough light to do anything but blink freely and scratch their noses. After a moment, Mary whispered, "What's taking them so long in there? And aren't they making kind of a lot of noise about it?"

"That door seems to muffle noise pretty well," said Alan, trying to listen.

Jane whispered, "The Master Toymaker has a very nice voice."

"You should hear him sing," Alan whispered. "Almost made up for having to hear him speechify."

Mary whispered, "At least your Uncle Barnaby tries to buy people's love, which gives them a little something material out of it, if not enough to make up for the rents he gouges out of them other days. The Toymaker just made it a law, that his people have got to love him or else."

"I wish you wouldn't talk that way about Uncle Barnaby," Jane whispered back.

"Shhh!" said Mary.

The office door was opening again.

But only the Toymaker and his Apprentice came out, each carrying a lamp. The Master Toymaker looked satisfied. Grumio looked worried. And where was Mr. Marmaduke?

Grumio was saying, "We... we aren't going to break them up right now, are we?"

"No. Presently. After I've attended to a more important matter, and have time to relax. For now, you can put them in the workroom."

"Mr. Marmaduke was the only one who could make his clockwork puppets move."

"Then carry them the old-fashioned way! I suppose you can still do that, Grumio? Use the trolley if you must. Now let me get back to first things first."

The Master Toymaker left through the hallway door. After a moment, Grumio slipped softly over, peeped out after him, nodded, and returned to the waiting three. "It's all right," he murmured, "for now. He's working on something he's got set up in the showroom."

"What is it?" murmured Mary, and Alan and Jane, "What's going on?" and "What's wrong?"

"He never wanted to see you act again," Grumio explained. "He wants to take you apart and see how you work. He bought you—"

"And Marmaduke sold us?" Alan said all but aloud.

"If he tries taking us apart," said Mary, "he's going to have a messy time of it."

"Mr. Marmaduke did the best he could not to sell you. He took the money thinking it was only for your performance. Then the Master wouldn't take it back, and called me to witness that he had just bought you, whether we'd known what it was all about, or not. When Marmaduke started making a fuss, Master opened his other office door, the one leading outside, where he had a couple of Court officials waiting to gag Marmaduke and wrestle him away."

"Wow," said Mary.

"Oh, dear!" breathed Jane.

"Now shall we run for it?" said Alan.

"Let me take you to the workroom, as ordered," said Grumio. "It has a door out to the necessary—this place is full of doors, takes me a little while to lock up every night—and you can get out that way. But I'd better take you one at a time, stiff on the trolley, so if he looks out of the showroom, he won't see you moving by yourselves and suspect something."

Alan pointed out, "He's bound to suspect something when he finds us gone."

"Well... I'll make it look like you've been puppet-napped or something, by somebody or other—"

"By ourselves, of course," said Mary.

"And once we're out of our costumes and make-up," said Jane, "nobody will recognize us—"

"If our luck holds," said Alan.

"And maybe better wait a day or two," said Grumio, "before applying for your passports out of Toyland."

"Now let's get down to the important business of escaping," said Alan. "Ladies first."

But even as Grumio went to fetch the trolley, there came a loud hammering at the back door, and a deep voice demanding to be let in.

"Uncle Barnaby!" said Jane.

Mary rolled up her eyes. "Will I never be rid of him?"

"How," Alan wondered, "can he even know we're here in the Toymaker's shop?"

"That's just the point," said Mary. "He can't. Or anyway shouldn't. It's just like he's my cruel fate and burden through life."

"Wait a minute," Jane remembered. "Hilda told us he wanted to start his search in Toyland because he also had some business to conduct here."

"Maybe going to try cutting a deal with the Toymaker again," Alan guessed. "To carry Toyland toys in Barnaby's Bodacious Bundles. Where, if the people of Barnabyville ever buy any toys at all, they'll buy the Master Toymaker of Toyland's toys."

"Better let him in before anything else," said Grumio, "or he'll disturb the Master."

Alan sat back down on the bench and froze into place before he noticed that Mary and Jane had retreated deeper into the shadows before taking up their clockwork automaton poses. Grumio was already opening the door to Uncle Barnaby.

"Where's your Master Toymaker?" said Uncle Barnaby.

"I'm afraid he's very busy at the moment, sir. Maybe you could come back tomorrow?"

"Too busy to do a little important business with his good neighbor, Mayor Barnaby of Barnabyville? Nonsense! Here—take this to him." Uncle Barnaby handed Grumio a bottle. "The best wine Bunberry has to offer. A little gift from me to my fellow Mayor, to sweeten our deal."

"I'll... try, Mr Barnaby. I'll see what he says, but I can't promise he'll see you tonight." Grumio took the wine and turned for the hallway.

Alan wondered whether his sister was wondering along with him why they shouldn't reveal themselves right now, when Uncle Barnaby stopped and stared down at him.

"Bad light in here," said Uncle Barnaby, "but this looks rather like one of those puppet automatons I saw today at Marmaduke's show."

"Yes, sir. My Master just bought it. To study its clockworks."

"Umph. Very well made." Uncle Barnaby prodded the supposed clockwork figure with his cane.

It's now or never, thought Alan.

Uncle Barnaby said, "Pity it looks so much like my worthless nephew."

Alan thought, stunned, It's never!

He held his lifeless-mannequin imitation while Uncle Barnaby shoved him off the bench, sat himself down, and snapped his fingers to hurry Grumio along.

Hey! At least be careful of my delicate clockwork!

Grumio hurried along. Even as his footsteps hurried down the hallway into silence, who should step in the back-alley door but Gonzorgo and Roderigo.

"What!" exclaimed Uncle Barnaby. "You two again?"

"And wanting our money," said Gonzorgo.

"No. Not one penny more. In fact, you owe me a refund, after the way you bungled drowning my niece and nephew."

"Well, we didn't fail you this last time," said Gonzorgo. "They'll never come out of Spider Forest."

Roderigo indulged a little of his famous sobbing.

About now the Master Toymaker himself came in. "What?" he cried, in pretty nearly the same tone Uncle Barnaby had just used. "You two? How could you have gotten rid of that Marmaduke fellow so quickly?"

"Jail's right over there in the Courthouse, isn't it?" said Gonzorgo.

Roderigo added, "And the Courthouse is just across the town square."

"My, my, my!" said the Toymaker. "Speaking as Mayor, we may not have made too bad a decision in hiring you. Even without references. But be off with you now. Grumio, time to lock up for the night. And then you can get those clockwork puppets into the workroom while I talk business with Mr. Barnaby."

"Yes, sir," said Grumio, who must have followed his master back into the storeroom. Not daring to move a muscle set even more of a limit than the bad light on what Alan could follow with his eyes.

After Gonzorgo and Roderigo had been shooed away, which might not have been that easy for Grumio to do all by himself if the Mayor of Toyland had not been there overseeing it, the Master Toymaker took Uncle Barnaby into his office, while Grumio went about locking up the building.

"I'll leave the outer workroom door on the latch," he murmured to the three, "so you'll still be able to get out all right once I trolley you into the workroom."

"But did you hear Uncle Barnaby?" Jane whispered, sounding as heartbroken as Alan felt. "Captain Gonzorgo and Mr. Roderigo, too. And we loved him, and trusted..."

Mary said, "I wish I could call myself surprised."

"All these years..." said Alan.

Mary added, " And that... man... wants to make me Mrs. Barnaby!"

"You could be right," Alan admitted sadly. "Nothing would surprise me now."

He had been wrong. There were still several bad surprises to come. The very worst of them was when she married Uncle Barnaby, after all.

CHAPTER XIII

But her marriage hadn't come until the following day—today. Maybe he could just skip over the rest of last night and get to the last good bit, just this morning... No, the flash-past wouldn't let him, no matter how close Gonzorgo and Roderigo had gotten. After that one little hiccup just now, it picked up where it had broken off.

Grumio wheeled Jane over to the workroom first, and then Mary, but before he got back for the last trip, Alan heard a rattling at the back door and froze into his imitation of a clockwork automaton just as Gonzorgo and Roderigo returned, having jimmied the lock. Men of many talents.

"Either we can bait Marmaduke back into our clutches with it," Gonzorgo was saying, "or, if losing him costs us our jobs here in Toyland, we can gut it and sell its valuable clockworks."

Roderigo snuffled. "It looks so much like a real young man."

"It isn't, so stop whining before someone hears you who shouldn't. Not that I much like listening to you, myself."

"It looks so much like... poor Alan Flinders! Zorgey, are you sure they couldn't have gotten out of Spider Forest?"

"Lucky as we were to get out, ourselves?"

"Yes, but... Who'd have thought they could ever come back from the Wooden Nickel, after all those holes we bored?"

"Well, I hope they're gone for good this time. Now stop sniveling and take its legs."

They started trying to pick Alan up. Maintaining his marionette posture, he made the by now well-practiced whirring noise in his throat and jerked out first one limb and then another, effectively blocking all their attempts.

"What started its works working?" wondered Gonzorgo.

"How do you turn him off?" asked Roderigo, trying to feel Alan all over. (Good thing Alan wasn't ticklish.)

He let them stand him up on his two legs and, as soon as he was in a good position to make it seem like more mechanical jerking, he uppercut Gonzorgo with one forearm, right away doubling over and driving his other elbow into Roderigo's big belly. Both men saying "Ouf!" at almost the same moment, they dropped Alan and retreated. He obligingly let his body fold to the floor and lay quietly crumpled.

"If I only had a hammer!" Gonzorgo almost shouted—but managed to keep his voice down. "See a hammer anywhere around here?"

"Somebody said there's a workroom across the hall," said Roderigo.

"Good. Should be hammers there, and saws and mallets."

"Only, only he looks so darn real! I wish he didn't look so real..."

(Even if they forgot Floretta the fawn of the forest, they almost had to have figured out by today that the last night's clockwork man was the same Alan they were about to execute.)

But as they made ready to drag Alan, still whirring and jerking his limbs, to the workroom (where he wasn't quite sure what he would do next), came the sound of the office door opening. Gonzorgo and Roderigo dropped everything else and scampered, vanishing out the back door just as the two Mayors emerged from the Master Toymaker's office.

"Hey, there! Stop!" the Master Toymaker shouted.

They did not. No matter how deep, resonant, and musical their Mayor's voice.

"What's going on?" said Uncle Barnaby. "Who was it?"

Alan had stopped whirring and jerking, and now lay perfectly if uncomfortably still.

"Children, probably," said the Toymaker. "Very bad children, but aren't they all?" In a lower voice, "If I only knew which ones they were, they wouldn't have to wait until Christmas to have a nasty surprise." Louder again, "Grumio!"

"Christmas," said Uncle Barnaby. "It's practically here. In just three or four months, it will be stomping all over us again."

"Grumio! Did I or did I not tell you to lock up?"

"I did, Master."

There was a short silence, during which Alan could imagine the Master Toymaker pointing to the outer door. Grumio's footsteps crossed over in that direction. Then: "Master, the lock's been jimmied."

"Go find another lock. There should be some in the workroom."

More footsteps. Halfway to the hallway, they paused. "Master, look at the clockwork puppet! Should I move—"

"Leave it as it is, Grumio, and go fetch that lock."

The footsteps went on and out of the room.

"Children!" said Uncle Barnaby. "Brats! Infernal little imps! What I wouldn't give to make them all suffer for the trouble they've given me!"

"To be exact," the Master Toymaker said in his melodious voice, "what would you give?"

Another pause. Uncle Barnaby must be eyeing the Toymaker. Likely looking thoughtful. "Quite a lot," he said at last. "Why?"

"I know of toys that injure, wound, and maim, for all their innocent appearance. People pay good money for them, believing them as harmless as they look. Why shouldn't someone buy them who knows otherwise?"

"Defective toys, you mean? How soon can I buy them?"

Another pause. A short one. Then the Master Toymaker said, "I think we may trust each other. You hate children. So do I. I loathe the little beasts! But I teach them to love me, so that they will accept from my hands the very playthings which will later wound and maim them."

"The very things for the Widow Piper's younger cherubs!" chortled Uncle Barnaby.

"A man after my own heart—oh, there you are, Grumio," the Master Toymaker went on more loudly.

"I have the new lock, Master."

"Good. Lock up now, and leave us. Mr. Barnaby and I will leave later, by my office door to the alley."

"Yes, Master. Master, what about the puppet? Shall I take him—I mean it—to the workroom with the others?"

"No, Grumio, leave it where it is. I thought I heard it whirring a bit, a minute ago, and saw it jerking a little. Those children who broke in must have started its works somehow, and I want to see what may happen if it's just left alone for a few hours. Now lock up and go home."

"Master... Yes, Master."

Alan's position on the floor just let him get a glimpse of Grumio's face as the Apprentice passed him. It was a very worried face.

"Master," said Grumio, "this one's a lock I can't lock from out-side. I'll have to go out through your office, myself."

"Go."

The Master Toymaker left no room for argument. Grumio had to go, and Alan was alone with the two Mayors, in an awkward and un-comfortable position that he could not break without giving himself away.

The Master Toymaker resumed, "Yes, I think that Barnaby's Bo-dacious Bundles may, after all, be the perfect business concern to help me distribute my very special toys."

"Good, good!" Uncle Barnaby was probably rubbing his hands together. "How soon can we expect our first shipment?"

"Soon. Any week now." The Master Toymaker coughed dryly. "You say you wish to see these infernal small beasts suffer? What would you say to more?

"More?"

"The ultimate."

"The ultimate in suffering? I'd say they merited it."

"A man after my own heart! Say the toys were more than merely dangerous—say that they were deadly? Not only maiming those who play with them, but killing."

"I'd double your commission." Uncle Barnaby said it without even hesitating.

"Good! Fine! Money gratifies the body as mischief gratifies the soul. And I can give a doll everything but a soul. Voice, movement, until it seems to live. As you perhaps saw today when my Clock-work Regiment paraded... What would you say to a doll that thinks thoughts like our own?"

"Like my thoughts and yours?"

"Exactly! A doll with the soul of a demon!"

"The soul of a demon," Uncle Barnaby repeated slowly. "Many dolls—an entire regiment of dolls—with the souls of demons! Yes, that would give these young brats of children their match... But how?" His voice sank half to a whisper. "Enchantment?"

"It has taken me years of patient toil, but I have at last a mys-tic compound which draws from the air all the evil souls and mali-cious thought-forms wandering abroad through it. A legion of them have I imprisoned in a flask. There must they remain, trapped like genii in a bottle, until I speak the spell which will free them—but free them only far enough to serve me as my slaves, carrying out my commands, wreaking my will. I shall command these demon souls to enter my dolls and mannequins. Then shall each toy become a fiend, and I—its master!"

"Wonderful!" breathed Uncle Barnaby.

"These demon dolls shall I scatter far and wide—gifts from the shop of the kindly Master Toymaker to the children who love him, disseminated through loving parents and other kindly grown-ups who buy them from his shop and place them underneath their Christmas trees. In each toy, the fiend will give no hint of its presence until the children sleep on Christmas Eve. Then each doll will creep from among the other presents which await Christmas dawn, and slay the child for whom it is meant!"

"Slay with what?" asked Uncle Barnaby.

"Ah! Do you suppose I have not planned for that? They are all character dolls—all of them, from those no taller than my hand to the soldiers of my Clockwork Regiment—and every costume calls for a weapon. Gypsies with poniards, Indians with tomahawks, leprechauns with shillelaghs, cavaliers with rapiers, pirates with cutlasses, soldiers with bayonets, kitchen chefs with cleavers—all, all will be well armed."

"Barnaby's Bodacious Bundles will carry as many as you send us! When will you give them life?"

"At once. This very night. All waits in readiness behind the closed shutters of my showroom."

"May I watch?"

"You may not."

"Promises to be a much better show than the one we sat through this afternoon. Say—what about those three clockwork marionettes? Will the demon deal include them?"

(Grateful that the girls were safely out of it—assuming they could at least trust Grumio—Alan listened more closely than ever.)

"No, it will include only toys of my own shop's manufacture. Those puppets seem to be the invention of an even greater genius than I—at clockwork, that is, and clockwork alone—and I shall enjoy dissecting them at my leisure, to study their inner workings. They are for my amusement, not the children's destruction."

"But why can't I watch you demonize the dolls?"

The Toymaker sank his voice to a mystic murmur. "No mortal ear but mine must hear the spell which makes the evil souls my slaves. Now leave me!"

"Well, success to you!" said Uncle Barnaby. And left the shop, apparently through the office. Alan heard the Toymaker shutting and locking the door after he was gone.

The young man wondered if he dared change his pose just a little, decided he'd better play things safe, and held still until he heard the Toymaker cross the storeroom and turn down the hallway to the showroom...

Now he rolled over and stretched... waited about one more minute (trying to count the seconds by his heartbeat), and then stole into the hallway.

All the interior doors were open. Maybe the Master Toymaker intended his spell to come down the hall and animate not just the toys in his showroom, but those in the rest of the building as well. Even the cats of the house now seemed shy of showing their noses.

Alan stopped to investigate the workroom, even whispering, "Jane? Mary? Grumio?" and tossing a tiny screw onto the floor. Nobody here... no currently alive person, anyway, only the rest of the Clockwork Regiment, crowded up around the walls, and a few unfinished toys on the tables. It looked like Grumio really had gotten the girls safely away.

What he'd heard surely gave Alan the right—maybe even the duty—to spy out what was going on here. Slinking on down the hallway, he crouched in the showroom door, and witnessed with all his might.

The showroom was lit only by two thick, dark candles (probably black), one at either end of the long counter, and one little blue flame beneath a flask in a warming-stand. Now clad in a dark robe with its hood pulled up, the Master Toymaker stood at the counter, his back to the open door. He seemed to be looking down at a huge old folio volume lying open before him, its edges visible to the right and left of his long sleeves.

The Master Toymaker put out his right hand, took the flask from its warming-stand, swirled it as if he were watching the thick liquid inside. By the movement of his hood, he nodded.

"Long enough, now," he intoned, "have ye brewed, my broth of evil spirits. Yea, this time shall ye serve me well!" Raising the flask high above his head, he seemed to consult his book before intoning more loudly, "Proserpina, Queen of the Lower World—by the mighty name of Moloch, I conjure thee, hear me!"

Outdoors—or was it outdoors?—the wind began to rise.

"In the dread name of Moloch the terrible and mighty," the Toymaker droned on, "grant me power over all the evil souls confined within this prison." Again he shook the flask slightly. "In sign and token that I am heard, may it glow with the fires of your ghostly kingdom!"

The contents of the flask turned a lambent, lurid, glowing, sickly green. The wind rose to gale force.

"Answered!" The Toymaker's shout rose above even the wind. "You hear and answer me!" Lifting his left hand to the mouth of the flask, he drew out its stopper. "Come forth! Come forth! All ye spirits of evil, I bid ye come forth and enter into all the figures I have fashioned in human shape and form, whatever be their size!"

The wind fairly shrieked. And the dolls—the dolls became alive... blinking their own eyes... stretching their limbs... beginning to clamber down from their shelves...

Shrieking with delight, the Master Toymaker spun around, caught sight of Alan—clearly mistook him, in delight and the poor light, for one of his own Clockwork Regiment. "Speak!" cried the Toymaker. "You live!"

"I live—" Alan shouted back—"and hate!"

CHAPTER XIV

But why hate? he wondered now, again. I don't think I ever in my life felt any real hate, until that moment last night. Only then, never before... and never since. Not even now. Not like I felt it then. Was it just the shock of knowing the truth about Uncle Barnaby, all at once and from his own mouth, and about the Master Toymaker, too? Or did some of the evil spirits take a shortcut through me on their way to find more toys in human form?

But now the flash-past had reached last night, it seemed to be mercilessly slowing down to a crawl, as the Master Toymaker's triumph faded to fear. For even as he tried to command them, the toys turned on him—smashing glass, overturning shelves, brandishing their weapons like a giant porcupine gone mad—

Was Alan part of it? Or one more of its targets, as another flesh-and-blood human being? None of its many weapons struck him, but the surge bore him relentlessly along... a mob of fierce and living demon dolls, against which there could be no resistance... nothing to do but stay on his feet and rush along with them, lest he fall and be trampled under their feet.

The Toymaker fled. The dolls followed. Large and small, they burst out of his ruined toyshop, surged up the streets of Toyland in hot pursuit. Here and there a window opened to show light briefly before banging shut again. Alan found himself running side by side with the real Captain of the Clockwork Regiment, the smaller dolls swarming marvelously about their feet, keeping up but never getting in the way.

"You're the one," said the Clockwork Captain, "who marched for me today."

"You—remember—that?" Alan could hardly speak for panting.

"Now I do. Remember. It comes back. Thank you."

"Did I—do all this?—Make 'em—revolt?"

"Yes."

"By—hating?"

"No. By being there. If he had been the only mortal, he would have made it work. You being there too, that freed us all the way. Gave us our own wills. Thank you."

"Can I—get away?"

"Desert?" said the Captain. "We would have to shoot you for desertion. He is the enemy."

"He—gave you—life."

"He wanted to make us his slaves. Like extra pieces of himself. That cannot be life." Never breaking stride, the Clockwork Captain caught Alan's arm and ran on.

"You're—making me—like a piece—of yourself!"

"We still need you," said the Captain. And they ran on.

Well, why not? The thought drummed through Alan's mind. The Master Toymaker is evil. And Uncle Barnaby is wicked—too bad he isn't here, too. Are all us grown-ups bad people? I don't think I like being a grown-up. But this is no army. It's a mob—a mob of demon dolls. All armed to the teeth. A mob against one man. An evil man. I don't like being part of a mob of demon dolls.

They reached the Master Toymaker's castle. The Toymaker made it inside. Drew up the drawbridge. The moat was nothing. Just decoration—a little toy moat. They splashed right through. The bigger dolls lifted the smaller ones up high—the smaller ones scrambled to the top of the wall—fiddled with levers and things—the little toy drawbridge was down, and they were inside. Swarming everywhere, looking for the Master Toymaker. Their enemy.

Now if ever was the time to get away—but the Clockwork Captain had Alan fast by one arm, and wouldn't let him loose.

The Master Toymaker had given them voices. They used them. A great shout rose from the northeast tower. The rest of the dolls attacked there. The Toymaker had the door fast closed. The dolls broke the lower windows, threw in flaming torches. Something started burning inside.

The Captain still had Alan tight by one arm. Other parts of the castle were already blazing. The fire clomb up the northeast tower. Clomb and clomb. The Master Toymaker appeared at the highest window, the room behind him full of flames.

He shrieked. He broke the window. Jumped out, still shrieking, his clothes aflame. Plummeted down to his death. To his death among the demon dolls. If the fall didn't kill him, if the fire didn't kill him, then they did. The Clockwork Captain let go Alan's arm and went to join them.

Alan stared around. The castle was burning everywhere. All he could do was head for the drawbridge and hope.

He took three steps, heard a roaring sound, looked up, saw a big burning beam coming down toward his head.

The Clockwork Captain stepped into its falling path. For just an instant, he looked at Alan, said, "Thank—" and the blazing beam bore him down to the ground.

Half blinded by smoke and tears, Alan stumbled to the open gate and staggered through to safety. Whatever safety was to be had in a Toyland gone mad.

CHAPTER XV

The rest of that night was a blur even in flash-past, but all the demon dolls—the entire mob-lot of them—perished along with the Master Toymaker, his workshop, and his castle. Alan was the sole survivor, and somehow or other made it to the comparative safety of Tom's room in the back of the Toyland Courthouse, where he slept until after ten, when he woke out of curiously tranquil dreams, to find Mary watching him.

She wore a purple silk turban with a sweeping peacock feather, a flowing flowered frock, and a cashmere shawl in cream fringed with crimson. She sat in a straight-backed chair.

"Where's Jane?" Alan asked. "Or am I still asleep and dreaming?"

"Silly!" She kissed his forehead. "Jane is safer than us, and once again I am Miss Edwina Flaffingdale, poetess of passion—purple poems for pale people—and you are my brother J. Egbert Flaffingdale, the aesthetic playwright. We have J. Egbert's suit all ready."

"The literary Flaffingdale family!" It had used to be a favorite childhood game, including Jane, Tom, and as many of the younger Pipers as learned to hand-print The Flaffingdale Review of Fine & Literary Arts, which coincidentally boasted a circulation the exact same number as its staff. "Where did our costumes come from?"

"Marmaduke's trunks. It's lucky he hadn't had a chance yet to put these on his life-sized marionettes for a show here in Toyland."

"Mr. Marmaduke! Is he safe, too?"

"Of course. He got away from Gonzorgo and Roderigo in about thirty seconds, and now that the Master Toymaker is dead..." a worried frown crossed her face... "nobody else except those two, us, and Grumio know Marmaduke was even there last night. And the Toymaker's cats—I think there must be more Toylanders claiming one of his cats found refuge with them, than he ever had cats to begin with. As it turns out, we can trust Grumio like one of us—he and Jill are sweet on each other. And that pretty pair Gonzorgo and Roderigo, who hire out to do anybody's dirty work, won't say anything about letting the puppeteer get away from them last night, for fear of showing themselves up as incompetent and losing their jobs here in Toyland. Anyway, Marmaduke is hiding out with my mother in her guest cottage two blocks from the Courthouse."

"Your mother! How much does—Did your whole family recognize us... was it only yesterday?"

"Mother knows everything, now. Including how your Uncle Barnaby has been trying all these years to do away with you and Jane and have your inheritance all to himself. I think it must have been the thought of being Barnaby's sister that did for your poor mother. Anyway. After Tom told Mother, just like that, he's all grown up now and on his own, I told her that what's sauce for the gander is sauce for the goose. And I think Jack and Jill are on the verge of breaking away, too. Now eat your breakfast, so you can get dressed."

Alan studied his tray, which held sausage, cheese, and a bun that looked like they came from Mr. Marmaduke's provisions. Also a generous slice of angel-food cake and a pot of Toyland's famous hot chocolate, steaming on a warming-stand. Innocent though it was, the warming-stand made Alan think of last night, so he snuffed out its candle before even starting on his bun and sausage. "Angel cake," he mused, regarding it again. "Like your mother used to make."

"She still does. This is hers—fortunately, the guest-cottage kitchen is well provided. Toyland angel cake is like everything else they make here—too sweet by more than half."

"Remember how we always said, if we ever got married, our wedding cake would be angel food?"

"If it wasn't devil's food." Mary nodded dreamily. "Far as I know, still goes."

"I'd rather you be Mrs. J. Edgar Flaffingdale this time."

"Well, I'm afraid that's impossible. Sisters don't marry brothers, you know, and to get passports for man and wife, we should need to present our marriage certificate at the Passport Office."

"But not a birth certificate for brother and sister?"

"Citizens of Toyland are required by Law to be too happy ever to leave their native city-state, because 'once you pass its borders, you can ne'er return again.' So only visitors can apply for passports out, and who ever travels with their birth certificates?"

"But they do with their marriage certificates?"

"Oh, yes! Wives are always ready everywhere to wave those at a moment's notice.[10] Now eat your breakfast."

"And the Passport Office is still doing business as usual, after last night?"

"The late Master Toymaker of lamented memory may have been the ultimate authority for everything in Toyland, but he had his flunkeys all in place to save him from having to handle the nitty-gritty details of everyday work. Toyland is stunned by what happened last night, even if they'll never know why it happened, but everything's still functioning as usual, with all the old, Toymaker-made and approved laws and procedures stuck fast in place. It wasn't the Courthouse that burned down, after all."

"How soon can I see Jane?"

"We'll try to dash in for a brother- and sisterly-kiss on our way out of Toyland."

"Back to Barnabyville, where I'll make Uncle Barnaby hand over Jane's and my inheritance."

"You and what army? Now the whole Clockwork Regiment is destroyed."

Yes, all Toyland would know that much, even if they didn't know how the toy soldiers and other dolls had been enlivened with the souls of demons. He told Mary all about it now.

"Oh, Alan!" she cried when he had finished. "How much that explains! Oh, my love, you mustn't blame yourself for what happened to that evil old man—think of all the children's lives you will have saved this Christmas!"

"Should we tell the rest of Toyland?"

Mary thought for several minutes before shaking her lovely head. "No... no, I think not. Even if we didn't have to keep your—I mean our—identities secret, it might be much better to leave Toylanders their dream, where he's an ideal of benevolence. Let them put up a statue of him in the town square, hang it with flowers in May and holly at Christmastime, and just quietly forget who was really responsible for the bad old laws when they replace them with good new ones of the kind they think he'd want."

10 It may be hard for us at the beginning of the 21st century to appreciate how vitally important it was for respectable Victorian and Edwardian wives to be able to prove they were legally married.

"Meanwhile, where is Jane now? Other than 'safer than we are.'"

"In the guest cottage. Mrs. Tom Piper, as she is now."

"Married? They got married!"

"It was the safest thing to do. Nobody will dare touch the wife of the Chief Courthouse Factotum, especially not just now, with Toyland itself functioning like a great clockwork automaton without its head."

"My sister Jane and your brother Tom! Just as we always expected! Wish I'd been there."

"Be comforted: that was a piece of their angel wedding cake you ate just now. And maybe someday we can do an encore performance for your especial benefit. They spent their honeymoon night in the bedroom Mother had ready for Tom anyway, there in her guest cottage. Tom didn't mind staying there for one night, when tonight he can be back snug in his own bedroom with Jane—now his and hers both."

"Where were they married?"

"In the Toyland Courthouse. The Marriage Bureau is right across the corridor from the Passport Office."

The Courthouse would have been closed until this morning, and they had spent last night... Alan decided that was Jane's and Tom's own business, now they were safely married, with a certificate to prove it. "So, why shouldn't we just dash over to the Marriage Bureau first, become Mr. and Mrs. J. Egbert Flaffingdale, and have a fresh new marriage certificate all ready to present at the Passport Office? Or have you already told everyone in Toyland that Edwina is J. Egbert's sister?"

"I haven't told anybody at all about the Flaffingdales yet. Outside my own immediate family, of course. But Edwina the poetess of passion could never actually marry a felon."

"A felon?"

Mary gave him a kiss on the forehead. "You see, love, Alan Flinders is under a rather serious cloud just at present. His dear, treacherous Uncle Barnaby"—she made her usual face at the name, and by this time, Alan agreed with it—"saw you at the head of last night's murderous mob of mechanical toys—"

"I was hardly at their head!"

"I merely report Uncle Barnaby's claim. Since nobody else had that good a view, not even his Toyland shop flunkey Mr. Horner, he is in effect the one and only witness. And since you're the only person, whether flesh or clockwork or otherwise animate, to have come out of it alive, you are wanted by all Toyland for the cold-blooded murder in fiery flames of its Mayor and Master Toymaker."

After a moment, Alan said, "So that's why J. Egbert Flafflingdale has to take my place today."

"Besides, J. Egbert and Edwina's marriage certificate would have the Flafflingdale names, and wouldn't really be legal for Mr. and Mrs. Alan and Mary Piper Flinders. But I see you're finished eating, so just step behind the dressing-screen and I'll toss J. Egbert's wardrobe over to you. You can use Tom's razor to shave your chin."

(But were those the real reasons she hadn't wanted to use that handy Marriage Bureau for herself and Alan?)

He was tying his new-to-him purple silk neckcloth (slightly frayed) in a knot befitting his conception of an aesthetic literary man, when Tom came in.

"Good, good," Tom said, nodding as he studied his old chum. "You don't look a bit like the police description."

"No one ever does," said Mary.

"Now," Tom went on, "I'll go call out the last 'Hear ye!' summonsing you to appear before the Court Toyal and say why you should not be condemned to die. If you even hear it, you'll naturally ignore it, because they'd condemn you as fast in presentia as they will in absentia, but that won't make any difference as long as J. Egbert and Edwina Flaffingdale can get their passports and be out of Toyland before any officers of the court can find that slippery customer, Alan Flinders, let alone apply the punishment prescribed by a time-honored ceremony polished up and passed into law by the Master Toymaker all of three years ago."

"Pity the M. T. isn't with us anymore," said Mary with a grimace. Then she chuckled. "Just when he and Uncle Barnaby looked as if they were beginning to hit it off so well together, too!"

"Well, so long," said Tom. "Give me three minutes' start, then go out by the back door, come in again through the front door, head straight for the Passport Office, and don't let the bogeymen bite!"

CHAPTER XVI

They gave him three minutes' start, went out by the back door, walked around the building slowly so as not to get out of breath, and went in again by the fancy front door of the Toyland Courthouse, acting like honest strangers without a care in the world beyond aesthetic literary angst. Their costumes turned a few heads, but mostly the Toylanders were looking at the closed Courtroom door and chattering about what was going on behind it, where the judges of Toyland, like marionettes wound up by the old Master Toymaker before his tragic demise, were busy trying and sentencing in absentia the supposed mastermind of last night's revolt.

The clerk at the Passport Office was a streaky-haired man with incipient jowls and a mischievous eye, which he cast over Miss Edwina Flaffingdale a little bit too appreciatively. "Mr. and Miss Flaffingdale," said he. "Yes, certainly, I quite understand why you might want to leave our fair city today. We've even had to turn away a few natives who thought they wanted to give up their citizenship and leave our portals forever, after last night."

"What happened last night," Alan told him steadily, "has nothing to do with why we happen to be leaving today. We are on a literary tour of this part of the world, and should have quit Toyland two days ago. Now we must hurry if we hope to be in time for our literary society's big meeting in Gotham."

Mary surreptitiously squeezed Alan's arm, like congratulations for a fib told well and smoothly.

"Well, well," said the clerk. "A pity if you can't stay to see us put Toyland back together after last night's tragedy. Or at least long enough to watch the execution of Alan Flinders, as soon as they catch him."

Still squeezing J. Edgar's arm, Edwina asked, "But suppose they can't find him? Will they execute him as they sentence him—in absentia?"

"Oh, they will apprehend him, no fear of that. If he'd tried to escape before committing the outrage, he might have done it. But today the gates of Toyland are locked fast, and the walls patrolled with the utmost care. True, by real citizens only, the Master Toymaker's wonderful Clockwork Regiment having perished, alas! along with him. But the real men are doubly watchful and eager to turn the criminal over to Toyland's new professional executioners."

(Who were Gonzorgo and Roderigo—who must have figured out by now the clockwork soldier that punched them really had been Alan.)

Miss Flaffingdale furnished all the necessary information about herself (most of it made up), and the clerk, with something very much like a leer (were all grown-ups bad?) said, "The poetess of passion, eh? That would be, I take it, purple passion?"

"Brother Edgar," said Edwina, "why don't I just leave you to finish up here, while I go and wait in the corridor outside?"

It took Alan longer than he might have hoped, especially now that Mary-as-Edwina was no longer there to distract the clerk. If strangers had needed passports to get into Toyland, of course, the Office could have checked its files and found no record of either Flaffingdale. As it was, Alan had only to manufacture a good many answers as to where they had stayed while in town (he thought that in this emergency Mother Piper wouldn't mind her name being used as their hostess) and so on.

When, half an hour later, he finally stepped into the corridor, with both precious passports in his pocket, he found Chief Court Factotum Tom standing in front of the Passport Office doorway, ringing his bell.

"Hear ye! Hear ye!" Tom proclaimed. "'The Court Toyal herewith finds the outlaw Alan Flinders guilty of the beloved Master Toymaker's death and the destruction of both his properties—to wit, his toyshop in town, with all his newest toys within, and his castle on the hill—and orders that he, the said Alan Flinders, be executed as soon as apprehended—'"

"Is there a reward?" That was Uncle Barnaby's voice. Yes, there he was, visible just beyond Tom's shoulder.

"If you mean that in a financial sense, Mr. Barnaby," Tom told him, "no, there is not. It is the duty of every good and conscientious citizen to assist the Law with no other reward than the warm glow of Doing the Right Thing."

"Even without pecuniary recompense, I must do my duty as a good and conscientious citizen," said Uncle Barnaby, "as well as Mayor of the neighboring town of Barnabyville. The man you seek is standing right behind you."

"Barnaby!" came Mary's outraged voice.

Tom spun around to look at Alan, who now saw that Mary stood beside Uncle Barnaby, wearing a thoroughly shocked face beneath her peacock feather.

All Alan could think to do was try to bluff it out. "Who is this man?" he asked through his nose, in his best literary-aesthetic tones, waving a languid finger at Uncle Barnaby.

"I am your unhappy uncle, as you very well know, you ungrateful rogue." Uncle Barnaby pulled out his pocket handkerchief and wiped his crocodile tears. "Your unhappy uncle, who raised you from an infant, and whose heart you have broken. Take him away. He has disgraced me enough."

Alan made a break for it. Hardly had he dodged around Tom, when Gonzorgo and Roderigo came up from somewhere and seized him. This time, in front of all the people in the crowded Courthouse corridor, they held him fast.

"Wait!" said Tom. "Let me finish reading it. 'That he be executed as soon as apprehended, according to the due process as enacted and prescribed in Toyland Law, unless he plead the Benefit of Widow."

"The Benefit of Widow?" echoed Alan, Mary, and almost everybody else.

"Yes," Tom explained. "It is an ancient and cherished Law of Toyland, older even than the mayoralty of our late, never-to-be-sufficiently lamented Master Toymaker. It is meant to assist a deserving class of citizens. Any widow, with or without a large family, may claim a condemned man for her next husband, and he shall be free as long as he supports and saves her from being a charge upon the state."

"I won't plead that benefit!" Alan declared. "I'll die rather than marry anybody else than Contrary Mary Piper."

Uncle Barnaby grinned. "If you mean Mrs. Barnaby, my darling bride, you're a little bit late in the day."

"What?" Alan felt as stunned as Mary looked.

"He promised!" she cried. "He swore and solemnly vowed, if I married him, he wouldn't 'recognize' you! Oh! The double-crossing rat!"

"My darling, my darling," Uncle Barnaby crooned, pawing her. "I wed you in purest love, but duty, duty must be done, though it breaks the heart twice over."

"I will plead that benefit!" said Alan. "Bring on your widows—I'll marry and live... just to square accounts with my dear Uncle Barnaby!"

Tom rang his bell. "Hear ye! Hear ye! Let all the widows of Toyland be summoned hither forthwith." Then he waved his arm, and half a dozen of his younger brothers and sisters stepped up from where they had been crowded behind bigger people in the wide corridor. "Run over and get Mother," he told them.

"But she's here," said Simon. "In the Courthouse."

Uncle Barnaby said, "I feel it is my painful duty to point out that the Widow Piper is a mere visitor to Toyland, and therefore no drain on this city's purse."

"Think I didn't check very carefully?" said Tom. "That ancient Law may have had only native Toyland widows in mind, and only needy ones at that—but it nowhere spells it out, and if they reword it next session, it'll still be too late for today. So Mother Piper will work as well as anybody."

"I know I work as well as anybody," said the Widow Piper, coming out of the Marriage Bureau across the corridor. "And several times harder than most. What do you want of me now, my grown-up son who is out on his own?"

"Mom, you've got to marry Alan and save his life!"

"Oh, dear!" said Mrs. Piper. "I can't."

"Mother!" cried Mary. "Never mind me! If you don't marry Alan, they're going to put him to death!"

"But it isn't a question of your prior claim, my lovely—and grown-up—daughter. I can't marry poor Alan because I am not the Widow Piper any longer. I've just become Mrs. Delancey Marmaduke. He's in there signing the marriage license right now."

Actually, he was just then stepping out into the corridor, one hand waving the license to dry the ink, and the other arm going around his bride as soon as he was close enough.

Alan remarked, "That Marriage License Bureau seems to be a busy place this morning. Why didn't you two couples notice each other in there?"

Mrs. Marmaduke said, "We two were in their rent-a-chapel in back, with a real parson, not just a justice of the peace. We wanted to make it as romantic as we could. Children, your new father simply swept me off my feet!"

"And Louisa simply swept me off mine," said Marmaduke. "There we were, both of us knocked flat on the floor, so we knew there was nothing for it but to get married right away."

Mary wailed, "But this is terrible! Mr. Marmaduke, couldn't you just run out and have a fatal accident right away?"

Marmaduke said, "Now, there's a lovely, loving thing to hear the first time your stepdaughter speaks to you as a stepdaughter."

"My dear," said Mrs. Marmaduke, "young as you still are, you may find this hard to believe, but romance hits us older folk every bit as hard as it hits you youngsters, and maybe even harder."

Uncle Barnaby said, "The very idea I have been trying to get across to her myself—Mother-in-law."

"A cross is right," Mary muttered darkly.

Mrs. Marmaduke looked from her oldest daughter to her new son-in-law and back again, said, "Oh, my poor, dear Mary!" and folded her into her arms.

Tom meanwhile called out another "Hear ye! Hear ye! I call all these gathered here present to go round up all the widows in Toyland and bring 'em here." In a much lower voice, he added to Alan, "Sorry, old chum. The Chief Court Factotum of Toyland is going to have to lock you up till they get here. But this sure throws a spike into Plan 'B.' I thought sure we had Mother Piper to fall back on."

After Tom regretfully locked Alan up, Mary came to the jail cell and called to him through the little barred window in the heavy door.

He must have been feeling bitter about things, because his response came out, "Yes, Mrs. Barnaby?"

"Oh, Alan, don't. I only did it to save you, and then he broke his solemn word—and now I've got to live with the brute till death do us part."

"I'm surprised the old double-crosser let you slip away to talk to me now."

"He didn't. That is, not exactly. He came far enough to see this locked and barred door between us, and then he said you couldn't frighten him, but he'll let us have this last talk as a special favor to a condemned man."

"Not exactly 'condemned,' when we find a nice widow to marry me."

"He'll still never let me see you again.... Alan, will you do me one teeny weeny favor?"

"I will if I can."

"Well, as you've got to marry in order to live, please don't marry any dashing, pretty widow who'll make you forget me."

"Oh! Do you think I could ever forget you?"

"Men are so fickle."

"I'm not."

"We're very young, Alan, and maybe we don't even know ourselves that well yet. Anyway, for my sake, please marry the ugliest, crossest, and most disagreeable widow of the lot. Then I'll know that every time you look at her, you'll think of me."

"Precious, don't you think a pleasant, pretty one would be an even better reminder of you?"

"No, because you'll remember how miserable I am with your wicked uncle."

"All right, angel, I'll do my best to find the worst. Anyway, she might be the most desperate and quickest to take me."

Tom came up, cutting into their talk. "I hate to break this up, people, but here's the first widow. Mary, I'm afraid you'll have to leave now."

She sighed, smiled, told Alan, "Remember," and left.

Gazing after her, Alan asked Tom, "Can you find me a drunken cross old thing with half a dozen mean dogs and cats and squalling brats?"

"Are you crazy?"

"To oblige Mary. What I described might just about equal Uncle Barnaby."

"Well," Tom said softly, "I didn't want to frighten my sister, but the girl outside is the only widow they can find. Seems the Master Toymaker interpreted that ancient Law to require as much marriage as possible, so there'd be plenty of children."

As Alan now understood, the Toymaker had wanted that many more to kill, after their parents had made him rich buying his deadly toys.

CHAPTER XVII

She was the very young, very pretty, and very tenor-intent Mrs. Horace, and her departure brought the flash-past to the present—what little remained of it, as Toyland's two Jailor-Executioners reached him where he sat on the determinedly wobbly (even though three-legged) jail-cell stool. He stood up shakily and said, "G—gentlemen?"

Gonzorgo coughed. "We're... we're in a very embarrassing position."

"And only you," said Roderigo, getting out his handkerchief, "can save us from becoming perfectly ridiculous."

"You're—" Alan began. But tempering his voice, he continued, "How so?"

Gonzorgo replied, "When we start to execute you, everybody is liable to laugh at us."

"I won't!" said Alan.

"But there's such a lot of it!" Roderigo wiped his eyes and blew his nose.

"Here." Gonzorgo held up a large document. "Just look at the warrant."

Alan took it. Right away, words jumped out at him. Fierce words, like "thumbscrew," "rack," pincers," branding irons." Sitting down again on the three-legged stool, he started reading it through word by word. "Ow! Oh! Ouch! All of that?"

Gonzorgo said, "It's supposed to fill up two hours exactly. But we're bound to bungle it, run it too short or too long, and screw things up along the way."

"We don't even know how to do half of it at all!" Roderigo sobbed. "We were going to practice in secret... work our way up from—" he sobbed aloud—"guinea pigs..."

"Poor guinea pigs!" said Alan.

"Probably the Toyland legislature will be changing it soon, now the Master Toymaker is gone," said Gonzorgo. "But not soon enough for us. And if they find out we fibbed about being experienced executioners, we'll lose these cushy jobs before they get even cushier."

"I weep for you," said Alan. "How can I help?"

Gonzorgo replied, "Since you've got to shuffle off this hard cold mortal coil anyway, maybe you'll allow us to send you our way? It'll be much faster than this." He bent and picked up the warrant, which had slipped through Alan's shaking fingers to the floor. "Much pleasanter for everyone concerned."

"Just... one question. Did she see this? Mary—that is, Mrs. Barnaby?"

"Poor girl! Oh, the poor girl!" sobbed Roderigo.

"She did," Gonzorgo explained. "It was what made up her mind to become Mrs. Barnaby. Which up until that moment, she'd been dead set against. You never saw a girl so dead set against becoming a bride!"

So she loved Alan—really loved him, had given up her whole life's happiness to try and spare him these next two hours. Maybe... maybe in the long run, poor Mary had the worst of the deal. Years and years being longer than two hours... but that was philosophy, and philosophy was no help at all when looking at two hours that'd seem like years and years.

"I'll go your way," said Alan.

"Wise boy!" Gonzorgo clapped him on the back.

"What is your way?"

"Let it be a surprise," said Gonzorgo.

"Easier that way," Roderigo agreed, finally putting away his handkerchief. "Now. What would you like in the way of a farewell luncheon?"

"Luncheon?"

"It'll be your last," Gonzorgo reassured him. "They already have the table set up. Below the scaffold, so you won't have to look at the equipment while you're eating. Leave that to the audience, and have anything you like. Anything that's readily available, of course. Something appropriate?"

All Alan could think of was nice, light, fluffy angel food. "I can't think of anything but angel cake. Mrs. Piper's—I mean Mrs. Marmaduke's—preferably."

"And a glass of wine?" Roderigo asked eagerly.

"A nice deep red vintage," Gonzorgo suggested. "Say... cherry. Yes, nice, red cherry wine to go with your white angel cake."

"Yes. That'll be all."

"Good! Fine! Perfect!" Gonzorgo rubbed his palms together. "Just five minutes, and someone will be back to lead you out."

Roderigo bent over and said in Alan's ear, "And don't worry. None of those things in the warrant are going to happen."

Except the hanging, Alan guessed. And maybe their way would be to "slip" and strike him hard over the head with the irons. It seemed a very long five minutes before someone—Tom—came to lead him out.

"There are times," said Tom, "I hate my job."

"I guess we all have our bad days."

"Yes, being grown up isn't quite the bowl of cherries we used to think it was going to be, back when we were kids. They're all out there. Jane, Mom, all the younger ones, Mary and her brand-new old husband—"

"Don't mention him to me. The moment is sour enough."

After one last, manly grip to his shoulder, Tom led him out to the town square of Toyland. Sure enough, there they all were, the youngest ones clustered closest to their mother and new stepfather—Bobby and Red, Tucker and Curly, B.B. and Muffy, Peter and Sallie, Simon and Bobbie, Jack and Jill—Jill standing hand in hand with Grumio. All in the front row, with the assorted citizens of Toyland grouped behind, ready and eager to be horrified. Jane stood waiting anxiously at one side of the little table below the scaffold. Mary, looking even more unhappy than Jane, was near the table's other side. Uncle Barnaby hovered right beside her, managing to look possessive, bereft, triumphant, and mournfully self-sacrificing, all at once, with his pocket handkerchief to his face in his best imitation of Roderigo. At least Roderigo's handkerchief really got wet.

The tray was sitting ready on the table: one large wedge of angel cake and one glass of sparkling red wine.

"Nephew, nephew!" said Uncle Barnaby. "How it wrenched my heart to have to finger you."

The Piper children booed him.

Barnaby turned on them. "It was my duty! And duty, duty must be done. Always remember that! Each one of us must at all times do our duty."

The children, Grumio, and not a few of the native Toylanders booed him again.

"But it was my duty," Barnaby repeated. "I had to do it!" As everybody turned away from him, he went on, "Ah, me! To meet such treatment as this—only for doing my solemn duty—how hard it is to bear! To bear up under such great stress as this, I must—simply must—have spirits!"

He seized the glass of wine and drained it off before anyone could stop him.

"Hey!" shouted Gonzorgo.

"Oh!" cried Roderigo. "Oh! Oh!—Too late!"

For Barnaby had drunk it down to the last drop. Setting the wineglass back on the table (missing the tray), he looked around oddly for just a second before lifting both hands to his throat as if he were choking.

Then he collapsed.

Overcome with sorrow, the old humbug! Alan thought, watching Tom and an assistant factotum bear him back into the Courthouse.

"This is serious—very serious!" Roderigo was blubbering at Alan's shoulder. "He drank up all your cherry wine—all the wine you should have drunk!"

"Can't you just bring me another glassful?"

"Not like that one! We used it all up—oh! What'll we do now? Zorgey, what'll we do now?"

Gonzorgo eyed first the Courthouse door, then Contrary Mary, then his fellow Executioner. "Start heating up the irons... very slowly. And you, Alan, start eating your cake... very, very slowly. As slowly as you possibly can."

Alan sat, took one bite, chewed it as slowly as he possibly could. It was very dry. When at last he swallowed, it went down clawing and scratching. He was about to ask for a glass of water, when the Courthouse door opened and Tom came out again, looking as though he was having a very hard time keeping his face sober and expressionless.

"Mrs. Barnaby!" he shouted in his best Chief Court Factotum voice. "Excessive grief has taken Mr. Barnaby from among us. You are a widow!"

"A widow! I'm a widow! It's the only good thing he ever did for anyone! Alan—oh, Alan, you're saved!" She turned and told all Toyland at the top of her voice, "He's a condemned man, and I claim him for my next husband, by the Benefit of Widow!"

And Alan was on his feet, and Mary was in his arms, hugging and kissing as hard as they could while Roderigo (for once not weeping) and Gonzorgo, Jane and Grumio, Marmaduke, the whole Piper clan and all of Toyland cheered around them.

EPILOGUE

Alan, Mary, Tom, and Jane soon figured out that Gonzorgo's and Roderigo's intended way to send Alan out was with strong, fast-acting poison, and in selfishly drinking what was meant to be his condemned nephew's last glass of wine, Barnaby quite unintentionally made it his own last glass of anything. In gratitude to the executioners whose incompetence had saved the day for them, the four young lovers kept the secret ever afterwards.

Jill Piper married Grumio, who became the new Master Toymaker, turning the Toyland branch of Barnaby's Bodacious Bundles into his workshop and salesroom, though he kept Mr. Horner on as bookkeeper. Among Grumio's first moves was abolishing the law that required people to visit his shop so many times a week. Now they could buy his (safe, sound, and sensible) toys just whenever they wanted. As soon as that was taken care of, the new Master Toymaker absolutely refused to have anything more to do with the mayoralty or any other part of the government.

The softening of its laws and penalties according to what Toylanders fondly imagined their late Master Toymaker would have wanted made Gonzorgo and Roderigo's jobs as executioners ever more nominal, leaving them plenty of free time to supplement their incomes however they desired. As long as no one went missing and no dead bodies turned up, no questions were asked, and Roderigo could cry to his sentimental heart's content.

After Tom had resigned his position as Chief Courthouse Factotum of Toyland, he and Jane wandered the world happily together for several years before settling down next door to Mr. and Mrs. Delancey Marmaduke and raising their children.

Alan and Mary settled in Barnabyville right away after their adventure, changing the town's name to Valleyvale, inaugurating popular elections (Simon Piper was the village's first elected mayor), and thereafter taking no part in running anything but their own business, the Valleyvale General Store (formerly the original branch of Barnaby's Bodacious Bundles), where they did a thriving business, Alan being a lot more popular as Mary's husband than he had been as Mr. Barnaby's nephew. His brother-in-law Grumio's safe, sound, and sensible toys, imported from Toyland and priced to fit any budget, were among the Valleyvale General Store's biggest sellers.

Among the other customers of the Valleyvale General Store, Mrs. Marmaduke's brood always bought plenty of (safe, sound, and sensible) toys for their (many, and genuinely cherished) nieces and nephews.

www.ingramcontent.com/pod-product-compliance
Lightning Source LLC
Chambersburg PA
CBHW022047170626
46808CB00003B/1395